ISBN: 979-8-218-64165-8

Any references to historical events, real people, or real places are used fictitiously. Names, characters, and places are products of the author's imagination.

BOOK ONE

EVIL ALLIANCE

CREATED & WRITTEN BY

JONATHAN SLADE

A big thanks to Chasadilla for all of the amazing art she did to help

bring the characters to life.

Created and Written By Jonathan Slade

Character Art By Chasadilla

Cover Art By Jonathan Slade

To the one who stood by my side entire time it took to get here,

Thank you

This is a work of fiction.

All similarities between real events or individuals are coincidence and are not intended.

This story includes some themes some may find disturbing or uncomfortable.

If you agree to these conditions you may proceed and embark on this journey.

PROLOGUE

Evil. Most of the time, this word is used for villains and those with rotten hearts who commit atrocious deeds. Under certain circumstances, it's used to describe a team of warriors gifted with powers and potentially dreadful misfortunes.

Karma, Devil, Luck, Curse, and Jinx.

These five are the core of this ragtag team known as the Evil Alliance.

These warriors have grown over two millennia over multiple generations. This story is about the fragmented 27th generation.

Chapter One

A rocky path echoes with three sets of footsteps, punctuated only by the occasional rock tumbling down the large hill. Three individuals climb up the uneven surface, kicking down dirt and pebbles while they aid each other on their climb.

"Come on, guys, you're so slow. We don't have much time before we have to go back to the group!" a boy yells from atop the hill, dusting off his loose-fitting jeans. The boy stands up straight, revealing his tall stature and pale skin. He scratches his head without disturbing the thick locks of wavy brown hair that covers his ears—the kind that looks like he ran his fingers through it several times without a brush or hair products.

"Carter, slow down. You're faster than us!" another boy shouts.

"Oh, come on, Logan. I know you can do better than that!"

Logan sighs and shakes his head while resuming his climb. Logan shares a similar appearance to Carter, just without the towering height and his hair brushed back more.

"Wait up! I don't normally climb steep hills in my free time like you two!" a girl shouts from below. She has long black hair, her clothes enhancing her spotless, smooth, coffee-colored skin.

"Jimena, who said me and Carter do this regularly?" Logan asks, turning around to face her.

"Yeah! Also, how are you out of breath? Aren't you the one who's been in choir class for how many years now? You sing so much you should have the greatest lung capacity out of us." Carter smirks looking back at her.

"Hey, was that an insult? Once I catch up to you, I'm gonna give you a piece of my mind!"

The two backtrack downward and help Jimena climb the hill. "We're almost there. It should be up around here," Carter says in a confident tone. The group travels upward, reaching the top faster together. Upon reaching the top, they step onto a small plateau filled with overgrown grass and weeds. The three look around while walking through the grass. "If we're not careful, we may run into some collectable monsters in this tall grass," Carter says before coming to a stop. He turns his head to focus on a single point—some gray within the sea of green. Carter raises his arm, pointing his finger to the gray area like a submarine periscope peering out of the grass. "Over there!" Carter says, getting the other two to turn their gaze. The three trudge through the thick grass approaching the spotted area. As they grow closer, the gray splotch of color takes shape into a stone mound covered in nature's green camouflage. They circle the pentagon-shaped structure, looking for a way in.

"Are you sure this is the place, Carter?" Jimena asks while rubbing her hand along the walls, some stone particles sticking to her fingertips. Carter stops at one of the sides and presses against the plants growing on the wall and they cave in, falling to the ground. He looks at the stone wall and gazes upon a doorway. The entry is made of smooth rocks with an engraving of a pentagon in the center. At each corner of the pentagon there is a symbol that has faded away with time.

"I'm sure. This is The Temple of the Evil Alliance," Carter says confidently with a smile. The other two walk over to Carter and look at the door.

"Explain to me why we came to a place called The Temple of the Evil Alliance?" Logan asks worryingly. "I'm all up for an adventure, but this sounds like a place worshipers come to, or at least a place filled with traps that kill people, like in movies."

"Audible gasp! How do you not know what this place is? This is where the powers of the Evil Alliance are given to those who are strong and brave enough to fight in great wars. We're not strong, but I thought it would be cool to see it in person," Carter says.

"Wait, we're brave?" Jimena whispers to herself.

"So is the outside the only thing, or is there a way through this stone wall that looks like a door?" Logan asks while feeling the edges of the doorway. Carter presses his hand against the symbol and holds it there.

"Well, that didn't work." Carter takes his hand off the symbol and looks at it.

"What? Did you expect something to happen?" Jimena asks.

"Well yeah, a little," he says while pushing against the cold stone. Carter presses his shoulder against the wall and pushes with his feet, sliding in the dirt.

"I don't think that's gonna do it, Carter," Logan says. Carter stops and sighs, placing his hand back on the symbol.

"Please … just open," Carter whispers to the door. The symbol begins to give off a faint glow. All three back away, slowly creeping through the thick grass. The stone wall sinks into the floor, opening up a dark room. They all shiver and shake off goosebumps. Carter takes a few steps forward to the door.

"Carter, what are you doing?! It could be a trap!" Logan shouts.

"If it is, then I'll just have to try my best to avoid it."

"Carter, we came and saw the temple, now let's go!" Jimena waves her arms in circles, trying to get his attention. Carter stops in front of the doorway, waits, and then takes a step into the darkness of the temple. He stands in place for a moment, waiting for something to happen. He then pulls out his phone and turns on the flashlight, looking around inside the room.

"It's okay; you can come in. Nothing's gonna get ya," Carter says. Logan and Jimena look at each other and shrug as they slowly approach the temple. Carter reaches out and pulls them inside. They stand in the center of the pentagon room. There are five murals, a short stone altar in front of each one, located in the five corners of the room. The altars are weathered and cracked with overgrown vines. The other two turn on their phone lights.

"Wow, this is something." Jimena stares at the murals, amazed by the designs. "The craftsmanship and detail in the murals are impeccable." She continues to admire the intricate designs of the ancient murals. Carter looks around and notices five small cracks in the ceiling with light piercing through, landing on each mural. Carter walks slowly over to a mural to inspect where the light hits it, noting a symbol of a scythe. Carter goes to each mural to see if the light is doing the same. He stops at the middle mural and observes it more closely.

"This is the mural of Karma." Carter looks at the mural of a faceless warrior wielding two swords, fending off unknown creatures. Jimena and Logan move to the altars to the left and right of Carter and investigate them. Carter looks at the stone altar beneath the mural. He gives it a blow, launching dust and dirt into the air. He moves his hand back and forth in front of his face, wafting away the dust, trying not to cough. He sees a pentagon with two swords engraved into it. As soon as places his hand on it, he hears a slam. He quickly looks to his left and right to see that Logan and Jimena also have their hands on the altars of the murals they're in front of. Carter spins around and sees the door shut itself. "Damn … What the hell?" Carter looks down and sees his legs aren't moving. Jimena and Logan turn to Carter.

"We told you something wasn't right!" Logan shouts.

"I know; you can yell at me later! Let's focus on getting out of here so you can kill me yourself instead of this place!" Carter says while trying to move. The three look toward the center. A rumble occurs, knocking the three off their feet. A star engraved in the floor lights up with a bright white glow. The glow begins to dim in two sections, leaving only three left glowing. Carter notices the glowing sections are the three that point at them. "We need to move now!" Carter yells. As he tries to get moving, he feels a sudden sharp pain as the glowing star has launched a line of light through his chest. He looks at his two friends to see they've received the same treatment. "Son of a—" The white line of light fades, breaks apart, and separates into multiple small orbs of light that begin to swirl around them. The lights spin faster and faster as they absorb into their skin, then they all black out.

Carter Shadson

Chapter Two

Carter's eyes open to a sea of white light. He looks around to see nothing but abyssal white in every direction. He gets to his feet and dusts himself off, then glances down at his feet to see he's standing on what looks like nothing.

"Oh crap, I messed up badly." Carter looks at his hands as they begin to shake. His breathing quickens as he turns around in a panic only to see a black flame sitting in the middle of the contrasting white void. He walks over to it while clenching his shaking fists to stare at the flame in fascination.

"Carter Shadson!" a deep voice booms from the void. Carter backs away from the flame, which grows as the white void begins to darken. "You have a power deep within, waiting to be unleashed!" The flame grows brighter and changes to a deep red as it floats into the air. The white void vanishes and is replaced by darkness. The only light is from the flame that illuminates Carter's face with a blood red ray. "Let the powers of Karma free you as you are reborn in a new chapter in the tale of time!" The flame launches itself at Carter, engulfing him. He screams out in pain as he falls to the ground and tries to roll. He tries to stand up, but struggles as the flame places a weight on him. He crawls along the invisible ground, digging his fingers deep into it, clenching his fists as he feels his body burn. He slams his fist on the ground and pushes upward, feeling the flame get lighter. Slowly, Carter gets to his feet, clenching his fists tight, the fire blasting off his body. The voice booms into Carter's ear once again. "Good! Now go forth and destroy those who would stand against you! Go forth and take down those who have done wrong and avenge those who have fallen! Go forth and awaken!"

Carter jolts up from the stone floor in a hot sweat, panting as he hears a loud ringing of a bell. He rubs his face, opens his eyes, and looks at Logan across from him on the floor.

"What the hell …?" Carter rubs his chest for a minute and then jumps up to his feet, feeling all over his chest where he was wounded by the beam of light. "What happened?" He looks at the floor and sees his phone making the bell sounds. He grabs it, quickly looking at the screen and noticing the alarm's title. "Oh crap. Guys, get up. We have to go." Carter shakes both Logan and Jimena, willing them to wake up. They get up, dazed and confused.

"What is it, Carter? What time is it?" Jimena asks with a yawn.

"Time for us to get the hell back or else we'll be in trouble!" Carter shouts while looking up to see the stone door has vanished. "Come on." Carter helps them both stand up straight and they exit the temple. "Let's take the slope over here!" Carter rushes over to the opposite direction they came up. The two follow and see the downhill slope that takes them all the way down.

"Are you crazy?!" Logan grabs Carter's shoulders.

"Look, this will take us down to the smoother section and then we can run the rest of the way." Carter jumps off the plateau and lands on the steep slope and slides his way down the hill.

"He's gonna get us killed," Logan says.

"Yeah, but he does have a good point," Jimena sits on the edge and pushes herself off down the slope. Logan shakes his head and does the same. Carter reaches the bottom first, then turns around and sees the other two reach the bottom not long after.

"Let's go!" Carter starts running and the other two follow. As they run, Carter notices the scenery flying past him a lot faster than normal. "Almost there, you guys!" The three keep running, and soon, they're passing single story houses made of logs. They keep running until they reach a building that looks like a recreational center. The three stop in front of a man wearing summer clothes, carrying a whistle and clipboard.

"We made it, Counselor Brian!" Logan says, wheezing.

"Ah, there you three are. We were getting worried. Jimena, your group will be out at the field, and you two can come with me," Counselor Brian says as he walks away. Jimena waves goodbye as she leaves the group, walking past a sign that reads *Aqua Gate Summer Camp*. Logan and Carter follow Brian, walking past other groups doing all sorts of summer camp activities, from large-scale freeze tag to a tournament of Go Fish. Carter reaches into his pocket and pulls out his phone to check the time. His eyes widen.

"What in the fresh craziness?" Carter stares at his phone in disbelief.

"What's wrong?" Logan asks, taking a peek at Carter's phone.

"My alarm went off at five o'clock, and it's only five-o-eight. I woke you guys up and made sure we were okay and we still made it here in only eight minutes."

Logan tilts his head. "That's weird. Even with us taking the shortcut, there's no way we could have made it here that quickly." Logan tries to make sense of it while counting with his fingers. As they follow Brian down the path, they see other boys running past them.

"Why is everyone in a hurry?" Logan asks a boy going past them.

"Today's activity is dodgeball!" the boy says. Both Carter and Logan look at each other and sigh. Brian leads them into a building where another camp counselor is pointing people to one

of two sides. Carter and Logan walk up to the counselor and wait

in a short line as they separate everyone until the counselor gets

to the two of them.

"All right. You, blue team," the counselor says, pointing at

Logan. "And you, red team." They look at each other and shrug

their shoulders.

"Hey, good luck. Don't be mad if I get you out!" Logan says

while walking over to his side.

"Oh, it's on now." Carter smirks as he lines up with the

other boys on his team. As the counselors quickly review the rules,

Logan and Carter get ready to focus on avoiding getting hit. The

whistle is blown and boys run up, grabbing dodgeballs and

throwing them at each other. This goes on for a moment with only

a few kids getting out.

A ball is thrown right at Carter. He turns his head at the last minute to see the ball and ducks just in time to dodge it. The ball instead hits someone behind him. Carter's eyes widen with a blank stare. He reaches his arm out, extending it in a random direction and a ball lands in his hand. A counselor calls it and the thrower is out. Carter stands up fully, looking at his hands. He stares in slight confusion, only to turn and look across at Logan as they both look at each other in shock. Logan raises his hand and a ball lands in his hand. He stares at the ball in disbelief, not fully acknowledging what just happened.

"Whoa, sick." Logan turns to the other team and throws the ball, which then sails through the air and hits a kid. Carter turns back to the blue team and takes the ball in his hand and throws it while jumping across the room at high speeds. The ball flies and smacks a kid in the arm. Carter looks down at his arm in amazement at what just happened. Kids resume play. One by one, kids get knocked out until it's Logan and Carter. Both boys stare at each other with a ball in each hand as they stand in front of each other, ready to have a western shootout with dodgeballs. The two launch balls through the air in every attempt to hit one another; some of the balls hit each other and bounce back. The crowd becomes invested and no longer cares about playing, only who is going to win this standoff. After several minutes, they stand opposite each other, breathing heavily. Carter takes one last breath and rushes toward the center line. Logan panics and throws his two balls. Carter throws one ball in the direction Logan is running. Logan jumps backward, dodging it only to turn his head and get a headshot from the other ball, falling to the ground after the blow. The crowd erupts as Carter stands triumphant. They continue playing games until the session is over and a bell rings, signifying that it's time for dinner. All the kids rush to the mess hall. Carter and Logan go to a bathroom to talk in private while they wait for Jimena.

"Sorry about your face," Carter says while patting Logan's back.

"Did you get that same feeling I did?" Logan asks Carter while he washes his face.

"That feeling that someone was telling you to move in a certain way?" Carter asks while taking his shirt off.

"Yeah, that feeling. Why are you taking your shirt off? Whoa, hey, hey!" Logan looks at Carter in surprise. "You weren't that muscular, were you?"

Carter looks at his body and inspects it closely, noticing the details of muscle definition. "No, definitely not." Carter places his hand on where the beam of light pierced him. He looks at the mirror and sees no wound, cut, nothing—only a scar on his chest from a previous incident. He grabs his shirt and tries to find a hole in it, but can't. "You felt like you got stabbed by that light too, right?"

"Yeah, it hurt like hell." Logan rubs where he got hit and then lifts his shirt up to see the same muscular effect on his body.

"We should go find Jimena and ask if she has the same symptoms as us," Carter says, dashing out the bathroom.

"Hey, don't just … Nevermind."

They start their search for Jimena within a sea of kids. "We may have to wait till we find a place to sit in the mess hall," Logan says while gazing at the hundreds of kids. The two join the crowd and make their way inside, getting their food and finding a small table to sit at. Logan spots Jimena and waves her down. She comes over to the table with her tray of food and sets it down across from Carter, but next to Logan.

"Hey. Do you guys feel like you have powers?" Jimena asks.

"Wow straight to it." Logan smirks. "Yes, we both did. We both got this feeling like something was telling us how to move to not get hit and where to catch the balls thrown at us."

"Did your muscular system improve?" Carter asks.

"Weird phrasing, but yes. I've never felt this strong before; it's weird."

"It is, and I'm assuming where you felt the beam of light pierce you there's no hole in your shirt, nor are there any remnants of a wound?" Carter points to his chest where he was hit.

"That's right," Jimena says with a nod.

Carter thinks to himself then looks at the two. "Then it seems none of us are dreaming, which can only mean … we may have been chosen as the new Evil Alliance generation."

Chapter Three

After a long, silent meal, the three wander outside and go far enough away from most of the population to a secluded back area. Logan starts walking around in circles, biting his nails and rubbing his head. Jimena grabs a hold of his arm and tries to get him to calm down.

Logan's face is stricken with fear as he asks, "What's happening to us?"

Jimena tightens her grip on his arm and looks into his eyes. "Nothing is wrong with us; we must just be high on adrenaline from that temple. That place was old. There was probably some weird chemical in there that makes our adrenaline spike. Right,

Carter?" She turns to Carter with concern across her face, hoping for some good news from her friend.

"I keep thinking that too, but all evidence points to the fact that we are the new Evil Alliance, but it doesn't make sense. You're supposed to have five people in the temple to get chosen," Carter says to himself.

"No way! That can't be. We're too young, we're too weak. We can't be the new Evil Alliance," Logan says, shaking himself free of Jimena's grip. He starts walking over to Carter, but Jimena grabs his shoulder, stopping him in place.

"Logan, calm down. There's no way we're it. There's only three of us. There has to be five, like Carter said. So without two more, we can't possibly be the new Evil Alliance. Right, Carter?" Jimena stares at Carter, who is smiling. "Carter? You okay?" They both look at Carter, who is laughing like a mad man.

"Oh man, this is too good. We have these powers now. Don't you see? We went into that shrine, we each stood in front of an altar, we all saw the bright lights, and were all experiencing these same effects. Enhanced strength, enhanced speed, more stamina, a freaking sixth sense. There's too much evidence saying we are the new Evil Alliance." He clenches his fists and looks at the other two. "I knew it! I've spent so much time looking for that dang temple, and where do I find it? In a city outside of Parabi called Aqua Gate. Whelp, this is just fantastic."

"You can't be serious, Carter. This is not a time to joke." Jimena stares at Carter with concern.

"I wonder how we summon our armor. Armor on! Power up! No, how about, suit up! Dang it!" Carter ignores Jimena and continues to shout more phrases while doing different poses.

"You idiot, now isn't the time to mess around!" Logan rushes toward Carter and swings his fist. Carter turns to see the fist coming toward his face.

Carter's body is quickly encased in a blood red flame as it wraps around his body tightly and breaks away just as fast as it appeared. Logan's fist makes contact with Carter's face. Carter gets knocked backward and spins the other way. Logan backs up, shaking his hand as he looks back at Carter. "What the hell just happened?"

Carter turns to the others while touching his face to find a red metal mask with a gunmetal gray X going across the eyes. The two look at Carter as he stands in a long black coat with a red trim. A metal plate covers his chest. His jeans have turned black, and he has a pair of black boots with red straps over his feet. "What the hell just happened? Oh, wow! I look awesome!"

"Your hair changed color. It's black with red streaks,"

Jimena says while approaching him and touching the new clothes.

Carter notices straps around his chest and follows them to

his back where he feels two handles. He takes hold of them and

pulls them out effortlessly. Two large knives. "Well, there's no

faking this. We are the Evil Alliance now," Carter says. The three

stand for a moment, letting that sink in, only to be broken by a

light chuckle.

"*Pffft,* those are your weapons? Two knives? Good luck

trying to save the world with those." Logan laughs. Carter turns to

face Logan, feeling a surge of annoyance and tightens his grip on

his blades. Just then, the blades double in size, forming two long

swords. Logan flinches backward and his body glows green,

revealing a set of armor. Logan looks at himself covered in blue

and green plated armor accented with silver like a medieval

knight. He touches his face, feeling a metal mask similar to

Carter's. His mask is more angular, with the sides going up past his face, forming sharp points like a winged helmet. Logan rubs his head, his hair having changed to a darker brown that matches the leather straps holding the armor to his body.

"Who's laughing now?" Carter smirks while looking at Logan. Carter turns his head and looks at his hands, holding the handles of the two swords—a pair black, square-like hilts with red accents and no crossguard. The right sword has an angled pommel, while the left is simply squared off. Carter stares at the shiny clean blades in silence. The blades retract to their smaller size and he slides them back into the sheathes on his back.

"Okay, so how did you guys do that?" Jimena asks.

"Well, mine was activated when Logan went to punch me. And he seemed to activate when he flinched after my blades doubled in size suddenly, so if I had to take a guess …" Carter bends down and picks up a rock, then swiftly turns to Jimena and launches it toward her. Before it makes contact, Jimena's body glows red and breaks free. The rock bounces off her now protected face, sending it flying in a random direction.

"What the hell, Carter?!" Jimena says.

"Sorry, just testing a theory that seems to be correct. Our armor appears out of our instinct to protect ourselves. But that could also just be because we're new to this. Maybe if we get more control over it, we can do it instinctively."

Both Logan and Carter turn to Jimena. Her mask has more curved shapes, with red as its main color with gray accents, the eyes looking like rounded butterfly wings. She wears a red and gold skirt connected to a lightweight short-sleeve shirt with rounded armor plates covering her shoulders with a chest piece in the style of a pitchfork. Her red boots are heavily armored with black and gray layered plates. Jimena looks at herself with her long, now red, hair flowing down the side of her head.

"Why does she have less armor than us, Carter?" Logan asks, trying to understand.

"If I remember correctly, our armor is a manifestation of ourselves. Or to put it in other words, how we view the armor we want or need." Carter walks over to Jimena and gets closer to her. "There were times you wished you could escape your home life, right?"

"Well, yeah. You know how my family is."

"So it's possible your armor is lighter in weight for higher mobility."

Carter backs away from her then points. "Jump."

"What? Why?"

Carter sighs, shaking his head. "Okay, all of us jump as high as you can at the same time. Ready? One, two, three!" Logan jumps, barely reaching a single story, while Carter goes higher at nearly two stories. Jimena jumps up the highest of the three, surpassing Carter's height by nearly a whole story. "Jackpot! Just as I predicted! Jimena's armor is less because she is supposed to be an agile fighter. By making her armor lighter, she can run faster and jump higher than us, and if need be, she can escape from a situation with ease."

Logan reaches to his lower back and pulls out a small hand axe. He spins it in his hand and the axe blades double in size. He taps the bottom of the handle and it extends into a long staff, turning the hand axe into a two-handed weapon of destruction. The green and silver blades are decorated in vines with four leaf clovers on them.

Jimena reaches to her back and pulls out a stick with three prongs melded together. She flips it in her hand and the stick expands into a full red and gold pitchfork. The elegant weapon retains its compatibility and lethality while still being a weapon of style.

"This is so cool!" Logan shouts, spinning in a circle to look at himself.

"So, um, how do we get this off?" Jimena asks.

Carter is about to say something when all three of them turn their heads to see a camp counselor standing there, looking at the three of them. "Hey, what are you doing out here— Oh no." He backs away slowly as he sees the three of them holding their weapons. He grabs his radio and shouts, "Code red, code red! This is not a drill. Code red, location: south patio." The counselor runs away. Soon, thousands of screams sound in the distance.

An intercom turns on nearby. "All kids return to designated areas. Repeat, all kids return to designated areas. Suspects have weapons."

"They shouldn't call us kids, considering we're basically all teenagers," Jimena says. "As I was saying, how do we take this stuff off?"

"I don't know. We'll figure it out on the way; we can't get

caught by anyone. We'll regroup later once things have calmed

down. For now, let's move," Carter says, giving his first orders as a

leader. The three take off in separate directions.

Jimena Adorus

Chapter Four

Logan jumps from tree to tree, trying to stay hidden despite his bulky metal armor. He stops to look around and he realizes there are no more trees to progress forward with.

"Damn!" He looks around and hops down to travel on foot. He lands, rolling into a sprint, dashing behind structures to stay hidden. He gazes out into the field of running teens. "Crap, this isn't helping. Carter said our armor activates when our protective instinct kicks in. So if our urge to hide were to kick in …" He walks out, his armor disappearing as he does, returning to his normal clothes. "That's convenient." Logan joins the crowd and runs toward the safe room, police sirens in the distance. He peeks outside the door and sees Jimena running, trying her best to hide with the crowd. Jimena trips and falls down. As she gets up, she sees a police officer get out of their car with their gun in hand and fires it at her. She's shoved down, but when she looks up, she sees Carter lying on top of her.

"Sorry about that." Carter stands up and pulls out his sword. "Run!" She gets up as fast as possible and starts running away. The officer aims and shoots at her again. Carter slides to the side and swings his sword, blocking the shot. The officer's eyes widen in disbelief. Carter dashes toward the officer as they shoot, getting hit by some while deflecting others. He stops in front of them, quickly slicing the gun in half, then kicks the officer to the ground.

"Hurry! Go, I got this!" Carter says to Jimena. She resumes running away, her armor disappearing as she does. More officers arrive on the scene, quickly readying their guns and aiming them at Carter. "Oh crap." He draws his other sword.

"Lower your weapons and get on the ground with your hands behind your head or we will open fire!" one of the officers shouts. Under the mask, Carter's face freezes in pure fear. He tries to look at the officers, but the lights of the cars are blinding his vision. He takes a step back. "Take another step and you will be resisting!" Carter takes another step, turning his body and getting ready to sprint. The officers unload their rounds. Carter swings his swords frantically, blocking as many shots as possible. More and more bullets slip past Carter's guard as they pierce his body. After the rain of fire ends, Carter stands bleeding, riddled with holes. Logan and Jimena watch from their respective areas. Carter stumbles forward, dropping his swords on the ground and falling over backward, a puddle of blood forming underneath him. Jimena covers her mouth, stifling a scream. Logan stares, trying to process the sight of his friend being killed in front of them.

An officer leans into their shoulder. "Target neutralized. Beginning search for the n-n-next s-s-suspect," the officer stutters. The officers cower as they see Carter stand up, blood dripping from the holes in his clothes. His head slowly rises to face the crowd of police. The blood puddle on the ground begins to sizzle away into nothing as if it was never there. Carter stumbles forward, picking up his swords off the ground. He regains his balance, wheezes, then tilts the blade of his sword and runs toward the officers.

"Open fire!" one officer yells. They are too late; Carter is already in front of them. He passes them, stabbing through the hood of one of the cars and dragging his sword through, jumping away soon after as it explodes, sending the police flying. Carter lands and sees all the police distracted by the explosion. He seizes the opportunity and runs away, heading to his designated safe room. An officer yells, "We need backup!"

Carter arrives at his safe room before he's seen by anyone. He leans against the side of the building, holding his leg where he got shot. He breathes heavily for a moment while looking down at the wound, where he notices a small hole where there was once a bigger one. His clothes and armor also seem less tattered, almost as if the fabrics were weaving themselves back together. He takes another breath and his armor fully disappears, returning him to normal. Carter stands up straight and walks into the room.

"You okay, Carter?!" a counselor asks, grabbing him and pulling him behind a wall of tables facing the door.

"I'm fine. There were gunshots, so I stayed put hiding until things calmed down," Carter says innocently. They take Carter to the rest of the kids located in another room, all huddled together. An hour passes and police officers come to each safe house to give the all-clear.

"The area is safe. You may now leave the rooms," an officer says. The counselors group all the kids together in a large field.

"Attention, everyone. We have called for the buses to come and pick everyone up!" a counselor says with a megaphone. "Until then, go and gather your things!" Everyone returns to their sleeping quarters and packs their bags. After a few moments, Carter leaves the main group of campers to look for the other two.

He walks around the summer camp looking, but can't find them. He then feels a sensation telling him to go in a certain direction, leading him to Jimena and Logan, talking in hushed whispers. Carter hides behind a wall and listens in.

"Do you think Carter brought us here just so he can get this power?" Jimena asks.

"No, he wouldn't do that. I don't think he expected this to happen to us, and if he knew this would have happened, he wouldn't have brought us along," Logan says.

"I know, but like … he knows a lot about this stuff, so maybe he just wanted something for himself, but he needed us just to accomplish it." As Jimena mutters these words, a dagger of emotions stabs Carter, his face full of defeat.

"Do they really think I wanted this to happen to us? I thought it would be cool to see the shrine, but not this," Carter whispers to himself while clenching his fists. He then moves from behind the wall to greet them. "Hey, guys."

"Oh my god, there you are!" Jimena walks over to Carter and pats him down, checking for wounds.

"Hey, I'm all good. I ain't gonna die already." Carter chuckles and watches some of the counselors come to the middle of the crowd of kids.

"All right, everybody, the buses are here! Take your stuff and get onto a bus. It doesn't matter which bus, just get on one!" a counselor yells out. The kids rush in, and soon, the buses roar down the road, leaving the summer camp behind them. Carter sits next to Logan and Jimena, who have already fallen asleep. He pulls out his phone and looks at the time and sees it's ten twenty-seven p.m. He gazes out at the moon and falls asleep, only to have his eyes rip open, feeling the bus come to a halt.

"All right, everyone, we are here. We have already contacted your parents to come and pick you up. Please head out and find your parents quickly. It looks like it might rain soon," a man says to all the half-awake kids. One by one, the people make their way to their parents. Logan and Jimena find their parents just before it starts to pour down with rain. "Hey, Carter, do you see your parents?"

"No, they wouldn't be here anyway."

"Why not?" the man asks.

"I live alone," Carter mumbles.

"Well … we got in contact with someone and they said they would be here." Carter walks outside of the bus and sees a woman with long golden hair standing in the rain, holding a towel and umbrella. The two make eye contact and the woman rushes over to Carter and quickly hugs him.

"Are you okay, Carter? Are you hurt anywhere?" The woman looks him over, holding the umbrella over them.

"Lola, I'm fine. I promise," Carter says while brushing off her hands.

"All teenagers say 'I'm fine' when they aren't fine." Lola stares him in the eyes, but Carter averts his gaze. "And that tells me I'm right. Come on, let's go get you warmed up."

Chapter Five

Lola and Carter sit across from each other in a diner, the rain still falling down in blankets outside. He's wrapped in the towel with his head lowered to the table. Lola stares at him for a moment, then sighs.

"Your brother called me earlier, asking how you were doing. He was trying to reach you, but I explained to him that you were away at summer camp, so you probably didn't have cell service up there, which is weird considering the camp isn't that far from the city," Lola says while picking up a menu.

An older man comes over to the table with a pen and paper in hand. "Hey, guys. The usual tonight?"

"No coffee today, Mike, just water. And I will do the two eggs and sausage combo. Keeping it light tonight," Lola says.

"Sounds good. And for you, Carter?"

"My usual late night is fine."

"Right on. I'll be back with your drinks in just a moment." Mike walks away to the back. Carter looks around in the red and white-colored diner to see there are no other customers except for an old man in the corner reading the paper.

"Man, it's been a while since we've eaten here so late." Lola smiles and looks over to Carter. "Hey, kiddo, what are you thinking about? You seem lost in thought."

Carter lifts his head up and looks at Lola. "How much do you know about the Evil Alliance?"

Her hair is parted to the side, her gentle face looking back at Carter. "You're back on this, huh?" Lola sighs, looking at Carter's face. "Well, I don't know too much about them that the general public doesn't already know. They were an ancient team of fighters who would protect humanity from any threats. I do know that the last generation was the most tragic. From rumors and

50

poor knowledge, it was said the last Karma killed their teammates.

I'm not sure why, or if it has any truth to it. I do know you have

been reading more of your father's research on the subject,

though." Lola sets a napkin on her lap.

Mike comes back with a glass of water and a mug of hot

cocoa with a dollop of whip cream on top. "We had some leftover

dark chocolate cocoa, so I made yours with that 'cause I know you

prefer it."

"Thanks, Mike." Carter smiles and takes a bite out of the

whipped cream before he mixes it into the cocoa.

"I will be back with your food in just a moment," Mike says,

then leaves.

"If you're trying to chase the legacy of your father's

research, I don't mind, but something like the Evil Alliance isn't

something you just happen upon." Lola takes a sip of her water.

"As your guardian and basically your only family left, I want to make sure you succeed. I understand you miss your parents, but there isn't much you can do now." Lola rubs her neck. "I'm sorry. I don't mean to put you down. I love you, Carter. You're like my son now. I've known you for just about your entire life." Lola grabs his hand and looks into his blue eyes. "You are a very bright kid. You and your brother have bright futures ahead of you. I just want what's best for you. I want to make sure your parents know I'm looking out for you." Mike brings two plates out, one with Lola's order and the other with two fluffy pancakes and a few pieces of sausage.

"Thank you, Mike," Carter says. Mike nods and walks off. The two eat their food in silence.

"Man, I can't believe it," Lola says randomly.

Carter looks up at her. "What?"

"I can't believe it's been so long since you were born. I remember when I used to tease your father about how you could have been my actual son if we didn't break up."

"Yeah, you loved messing with him."

"Well, yeah, 'cause we split amicably and were still great friends." Lola giggles. "Your mother joined in sometimes, which made it even better." The two laugh and recall stories of the past as they finish eating. "Come on, let's go home." The two leave a tip, pay the bill and go home at four in the morning. They pull up to a house and park on the side of the road. Carter gets out and looks to the sky, feeling the lack of rain from the cloudy sky.

"So, does tonight count as our weekly meetup?" Carter asks while looking at Lola.

"No, it does not. No matter what we're doing during the week, you are required to meet up with me once a week at my house. That's our agreement for letting you live on your own."

Lola points at him with a stern look.

"Okay, I understand. Saturday?"

"No, Sunday. Before school starts up,"

"All-righty, then. Have a good night, Lola."

"Goodnight, Carter. Make sure to have all your stuff for

school ready."

"I will, don't worry." Carter shuts the car door and walks up

the stone path to his front door. He turns, waves goodbye to Lola,

and goes into his house. The dark home is illuminated by the oven

and microwave clocks and a small night light in the corner of the

room. Carter swings his arm up, smacking the light switch. He

shuts his eyes quickly, then slowly inches them open, letting his

eyes acclimate to the bright lights. He stands in the center of the

room and looks at his hands. He closes his eyes, then opens them

back up, activating his armor in the process. He turns his gaze to a window and sees his reflection. "This is the new me. There's no going back." Carter deactivates his armor while walking to his bedroom. He takes off his shirt and lies down in his bed, moving a thin gray blanket on top of his body. He stares at the roof, lost in thought. *What have I gotten myself into?*

Logan Stone

Chapter Six

A ringing goes off and Carter reaches out, grabbing his phone to silence the alarm. He flips back over, looking out a window at the sun creeping through the curtain. He stretches his arms up and gets a whiff of his own smell.

"Oh god, that's terrible. I could definitely use a refresh." After a shower, he dries off and heads toward his closet, grabbing clothes to get dressed for the day. As Carter is getting changed, his phone rings. He walks over to it, answering it instantly. "Hey, what's up? No, I'm not. Why? Sure, I can meet you there. Just give me a minute and I'll head out." Carter ends the conversation and tidies up his clothes, then walks into his kitchen, looking at the clock. "It's nine twenty-two? Yeah, they should be open."

Carter walks over to the front door and pulls two sets of keys off a shelf. In the garage, Carter opens the garage door, letting light burst into the dark room. The light slowly reveals a motorcycle and a car covered in a large blue tarp. He grabs the helmet, hops on onto the motorcycle, and backs out of the driveway. As Carter rides down the streets, he passes by a large school. He stops and looks at one of the signs that read: *Welcome to Castle High School.*

"That's such a stupid name. Most schools have better names, or at least ones that don't sound so childish." Carter shakes his head and rides on, soon arriving in front of a mall. He parks his bike in a designated area and hooks his helmet to his belt loop, then heads inside the mall. He makes his way to the food court, window shopping as he walks, but his sixth sense keeps nagging him, causing Carter to look forward and dodge people after almost running into them. Carter bumps into someone while trying to dodge another person.

"Oh geez, I'm sorry. I didn't see where I was going," Carter says while turning to the person he bumped into. His eyes meet with a girl's bronze yellow eyes. He extends his hand out to them. The girl takes it and Carter pulls her up to her feet.

"I'm sorry again," Carter says with a smile. The girl smiles back and begins to laugh, giving him a light jab on his shoulder.

"You may be tall but you still seem to run into everything, you big goof," the girl says while adjusting her small red purse. Carter smirks and gives the girl a proper hug.

"Hi, Dawn. How are you doing?" Carter asks.

Dawn brushes her long brown hair behind her ear, letting her russet face meet with Carter's paleness. "Pretty good. You got here quickly."

"Well, when you said you were at the mall, I thought I could use hanging out with you as an excuse to buy a new backpack for the school year, since my old one is pretty worn out."

"Aww, you're not her just to see little ol' me?" Dawn moves closer to Carter, not breaking eye contact. Carter smiles a little and grabs her shoulder.

 "So, clearly meeting at the food court means you want food, right? What do you wanna eat? I could use some fuel myself." Carter grabs Dawn's hand and pulls her along to the different food places. He asks at every store if she would like to eat there until they both agree on a place and order their food.

"Are you paying for the food, Carter?" Dawn asks, looking up at him innocently.

"Why should I pay for your food? Your father owns a multi-million dollar business. You guys have more money than you know what to do with. Your allowance alone is more than what I have ever owned."

"That doesn't mean a girl doesn't like being treated by a boy every once in a while." Dawn turns her gaze away for a moment. "Plus, I don't have my wallet on me."

"Oh yeah? Then how did you get that purse?" Carter says while paying for the food. Dawn looks at the red purse slung over her shoulder.

"I— What? How did you know?!" Dawn crosses her arms. Carter looks her in the eyes and grabs her cheek. "You left the tag on, silly." He then takes their food and begins walking away. "Come on, slowpoke." Dawn rubs the pinched cheek and grows flush red. She catches up to Carter as they both sit down at a two-person table. They begin to partake in their recent purchase.

"Are you ready to go to school?" Dawn asks in between bites.

"Not really. I feel like I didn't get much done this summer," Carter says, looking at his right hand holding a plastic knife like he would his sword.

"Well, we should be getting Ms. Morris this year because she's the only world history teacher anymore, so you should have an easy time."

"Why do you call her that? You know her as Lola, so call her that," Carter says.

"'Cause it's rude to call a teacher by their first name regardless of your relationship to them. So if I call her Ms. Morris, you have to as well. Even if you're kind of her son." Dawn finishes her food and preps it for the trash. Carter finishes just after her. He stares off for a moment until his vision starts to turn black and white. He feels his brain tugging on his body to turn the other way. He looks around until he spots a man highlighted in red, making him stand out. The man is wearing a medical mask over his face and a hat with all their hair tucked in. He has his hand packed into his jacket.

"Give me a sec to throw out the trash." Carter stands up and starts walking to a trash can further away from the table, but in the direction of the man. The sounds around him fade into one solid mumble. He gets close enough and bumps into the man. The man stumbles and a hand gun falls out of his jacket. As the gun hits the floor, the color returns to Carter's vision and the volume of the food court returns.

"*Gun!*" a girl screams. Soon, a massive uproar begins as the man reaches to the floor to pick up his weapon. Carter quickly kicks the man's face, knocking him to the floor. Carter grabs the gun and disarms it by removing the magazine and extra bullet already prepared to fire. The man gets up and pulls out a knife, pointing it toward Carter. He screams and rushes Carter, swinging at him.

He's so slow. Carter catches the man's hand holding the knife. He pulls down his mask for a second and spits at Carter's eyes.

"Eww, gross!" Carter wipes the spit out of his eyes with his other hand. The man drops the knife, catches it in his other hand and swings it at Carter again. His eyes dart open in fear as Carter dodges most of the swings until he tries to grab the other hand and receives a slice across his right forearm. Carter grunts at the slice. He turns his gaze back to the man and rushes at him. The man's eyes widen as he receives a blow to his stomach from Carter's fist. The man grunts and loses his balance.

The man drops the knife out of one hand and into the other, then lunges toward Carter. Carter's other hand moves faster than the man expected, and soon, both of his hands are held hostage by Carter's grip. Carter looks into the man's eyes and his vision becomes monochromatic again as he sees visions of the man causing harm to others. In one of the visions, the man chokes

out a woman and breaks her legs with a pipe. Carter's vision

returns as the man begins to shake and a loud clicking noise can

be heard. Carter looks up and sees Dawn holding a taser in her

hand. He sets down the newly incapacitated man.

"Carter, your arm!"

Carter looks at the wound and sees it heal slowly while

Dawn looks at it. His hand begins twitching as if it was being

restrained. He pulls his arm away from Dawn. "It looks worse than

it is." He quickly covers the wound with his hand. Mall security

finally shows up and starts questioning people and defusing the

situation. After taking the man into custody, security comes over

to Carter and asks if he needs medical attention. Carter shakes his

head and says he'll just clean it and wrap it up.

"You scared me! Why would you fight that man? You could have gotten killed! Lola is gonna be mad at you for doing something this reckless!" Dawn hugs Carter tight.

"Hey, I need to breathe or you're going to have to explain to Lola that you killed me," Carter says with his arms up. Dawn lets go of him, backing up slowly. The two go to the bathroom, with Dawn insisting on the family bathroom so she can clean the wound. "I told you, Dawn, it's not that bad."

"Carter, your whole arm is covered in blood. That's not something that just happens," Dawn says while rubbing water over Carter's arm in the sink. Dawn notices the cut is smaller. "I guess you're right. The blood definitely made it look bigger." Dawn digs through her purse and pulls out a bandaid and places it on the cut.

"How is there that much stuff in there already if you just got it?" Carter's eyes grow wide after hearing her rummage through the bag.

"Trade secret." Dawn smoothes out the bandaid on his arm. "Well, it doesn't cover it very much, but it can do the job until we find something better. Wait a minute! Let's go to the store my father added here. They're bound to have some medical stuff. We do sell some, after all!" Dawn rushes out of the bathroom, grabbing Carter's hands.

"Dawn, my arm!" Carter shouts while being dragged along.

"Sorry!" Dawn pulls Carter along like a wagon. They travel all over the mall until they reach a store with a *coming soon* sign over the words *Iron Works Outlet*. Dawn looks inside and sees lots of workers preparing the store. One of the workers notices the two and walks over, unlocking and opening the door.

"Hello, Lady Dawn. Your father was actually about to come looking for you. Please, come inside." The worker opens the door and lets the two inside.

"Father!" Dawn shouts. A man bursts from around the corner and rushes over to Dawn, picking her up.

"There's my girl! I was just looking for you. We're leaving soon, so I hope you did your shopping," her father says gleefully. He sets her down and looks at Carter. "Carter, what happened to you?" He sticks his hand out and grabs Carter's arm.

"It's good to see you, Mr. Shardlow," Carter says awkwardly. Mr. Shardlow looks at Carter's wound and calls for one of the workers to bring out the med kit. Mere seconds later, someone brings it out and sets it on a table. Mr. Shardlow opens it up, pulls out supplies, then properly cleans and wraps the wound. "Thanks."

"You're welcome, Carter. You should be good in a day. I put

on a cream I use for my employees that helps boost the

regenerative ability of your cells. We are trying to get the

properties to work faster to help aid our soldiers and make it a

more viable option." Mr. Shardlow smiles, then looks at Carter's

helmet, strapped to his side. "Carter, is having your helmet like

that comfortable?"

"I wouldn't say it's comfortable, more that it does the job,"

Carter says while patting the helmet. Mr. Shardlow calls out to one

of the employees, and they hand him an object.

"Here, try this on."

Carter grabs what looks like a curved metal brick.

"Now shake it!" Mr. Shardlow says with the excitement of

a child.

Carter shrugs and gives it a shake. The metal brick unfolds

quickly into a full motorcycle helmet. "Whoa!"

"I know, right?" Mr. Shardlow dances in place. "This is the quality of inventive products you can get from the Iron Works Outlet!" he says, standing like a president in a painting. "You take it and use it and let me know how it is. It's on the house."

"No, I can't take this. Really, let me pay for it."

"No, I insist. You won't take my daughter's hand in marriage, so at least take this," he says plainly.

Dawn's face becomes beet red. "Father!"

"Look, I know you want what's best for your daughter, but I don't have anything to offer her. Plus, I need to focus on… I'm not ready for a relationship. I'm still a little broken after my last one."

"I understand, but once you're ready, feel free to take my daughter." Mr. Shardlow chuckles. "All right, Dawn, we are done for the day. Let's head to the car."

The employee from before comes back out, holding a tablet. "Mr. Shardlow, I just got word back from the development team. They've finished the prototypes for the footprint security mats and are requesting you stop by to view the results."

"Footprint security mats?" Carter tilts his head, looking at Mr. Shardlow. "I know you said last time we spoke you were looking into the home security business, but what would footprint mats be useful for?"

"Well, those mats in particular are not for home security, per se. The mats are more for business' inner workings. Kinda like inner loss prevention, employee theft, that kinda stuff. For the most part, they're meant as an additional identifier. For example, most of my employees won't be told about it as a matter of security. But the mats aren't complete without the identifier cameras, and I'm going on a tangent about something that isn't fully ready or if it would even be of any use. Anyway, goodbye again, Carter. I hope to see you soon, and if you wish to stop by the headquarters to check things out, you're always welcome."

They say their final goodbyes and Carter parts ways with the two. He pulls out his phone and taps the screen a few times, then puts it up to his ear.

"Hello?"

"Hey, Jimena. Are you working today?" Carter asks.

"I'm working right now. Why?"

"I'm at the mall to pick up a new backpack. Want me to take you home?" he asks.

"I get off in an hour and a half. Stop by when you're done."

"All right, see you in a bit." Carter slides his phone into his pocket and makes his way through the mall. He makes a stop on the way to Jimena's work and purchases a new red backpack. Then he heads to the opposite side of the mall and stops in front of a shoe store called *Chasadilla's*. He walks in and is greeted by two female employees.

"Hi, welcome to Chasadilla's," they both say at the same time.

"Hi, where's Jimena?" Carter asks.

"She's helping a customer at the moment. Are you a friend of hers?" one girl asks.

"Yes. She told me she gets off work soon, so I came by to pick her up," Carter says. Jimena comes around the corner.

"Speak of the devil," her coworker jokes.

"Hey, Carter. Give me just a few more minutes and then we can head out," Jimena says, then heads to the back. Carter shrugs and steps outside to wait for Jimena to finish work. He pulls out a coin and tries to roll it across his knuckles, only getting two fingers in before it falls off and he catches it while his eyes lock on the collapsible helmet in his other hand. He looks at the Iron Works logo engraved into one of the inside sections of the helmet. He rubs his thumb over it. It shocks him and it runs its way up to his brain, flashing a momentary image in his head.

"You okay, Carter?" Jimena pats his shoulder. Carter's head jerks to face her. "Yeah, just lost in thought." He stands up straight and looks at her. "Ready?"

"Yep. Let's get out of here." She notices Carter's arm and furrows her brow. "What happened here?"

"Oh, there was some conflict in the mall and I got sliced. Dawn was around, so I couldn't heal the wound in front of her."

"How'd you manage to stop the healing process?"

"It wasn't easy. I just kept thinking *don't heal*, and it stopped, but the second I stopped focusing on it, it would try to heal itself," Carter says. "Put this on when we get outside." He tosses her his helmet. "Let's go." The two leave the mall and Carter leads Jimena to his motorcycle; he sits down and starts it up. "Get on."

Jimena hops on behind him. "What about you? Don't you have an extra helmet?"

"Don't worry about me." Carter smirks and expands the new helmet, then quickly puts it on. "Hold on." Carter revs the engine and the two take off. They decide to stop at a fast-food joint, parking and walking up to its outside dining area with a separate ordering window. Jimena orders her food and the two wait at a table for the number to be called.

"What are you going to do now?" Jimena asks randomly.

"What do you mean?"

"We have these powers now, so are you going to use them for good or for—"

"Evil? No, we were given these powers to stop bad people, so that's exactly what I'll do."

"Aren't you afraid of dying, though?"

"Of course I am. There's no way I wouldn't be scared. This is just something I have to do now, and I will embrace it," Carter says.

"But it's not something you have to do. The world has been doing just fine without the Evil Alliance. There's nothing we really need to do."

"Not to mention the reputation of the Evil Alliance is on the decline because of the previous generation," Carter says, rubbing his chin.

"Carter, I know this is like a fantasy for you, but we are not superheroes. We shouldn't get too involved. Nothing good will come of it."

"You're right, but I don't think I could just sit there and watch," Carter says, clenching his fists.

"And that's what is gonna get you killed."

"Why are you just pointing at me? Throw some flak at Logan."

"'Cause I know Logan isn't gonna run around chasing after every little rodent who commits a crime."

"Order one-fifteen, your food is ready!" the man behind the counter shouts. Carter walks up, grabs the tray and brings it to their table. Jimena takes her food and begins to eat. He reflects on his actions earlier at the mall.

"Look, Carter, you don't need to think too hard about it. If you see something dangerous going on, just think: would a normal person be able to stop this? If yes, go right ahead, if no, then just act like everyone else."

Carter clenches his fist tighter, then takes a deep breath. "You say that like it's super easy to just ignore everything." Carter sighs.

Jimena finishes her food and then puts her hand on one of his. "If we are needed by the world, we will help in any way we can, but in the meantime, just relax and try to enjoy your life before you get sucked up into a life you may end up regretting, because all this hero stuff is just gonna hurt yourself and others. What would your brother think if he saw you risking your life every day for random people?" Jimena looks into his eyes.

"You act like I've spoken to him recently. I haven't said a single word to him in almost a year."

"And whose fault is that?"

"Both of ours, 'cause neither of us talk to each other. He talks to Lola more often. She says it's sometimes just to check in on me." Carter slides his hand out from under Jimena's.

"All right. Let's go; we can talk more later." The two hit the road once again. After a few minutes, Carter pulls up to Jimena's house.

"I'll take that." Carter takes the helmet off her head.

"Thanks, Carter. I appreciate it. See ya later." Jimena heads to her front door, then stops abruptly and walks back over to him. "Please consider what I talked to you about. You and Logan are my only real friends, and I would hate to lose either of you." She smiles and walks back to her door.

"Later." He drives off, heading home. He parks his motorcycle inside the garage and goes inside, only to find an unfamiliar man dressed in what can be described as generic office attire standing there, looking at items spread across the kitchen table. Without thinking, he leaps through the air and swings his leg toward the man. Without making contact with anything Carter finds himself on the other side of the room. "Who are you and what do you want?"

The man turns toward Carter, his face calm. "Relax, Carter. I'm not here to hurt you, I couldn't even if I wanted to."

"How do you know my name?"

"I would say I am a mind reader and I have millennia of magic experience, but you left your mail on the table. My name is Leonidas. I am the soul of the Evil Alliance. I have been around since the day it was founded. I am nothing more than a specter, a visual for you to see so you don't think you're going insane."

Carter keeps his fists clenched while walking slowly around Leonidas. "Is there something you need from me?"

"Look, I get it. Some random person just shows up in your house and you're on edge. Go ahead and use your equal vision and you will see nothing on me."

"My what?"

"As Karma, your powers comprise equality and or fairness. Another way to think about it is equivalent exchange. You're able to see the damage others do and give them the same pain back. That vision of yours can only detect physical living beings, but a

80

specter like myself cannot be detected." Carter activates his armor and pulls out one of his swords, throwing it toward Leonidas. The blade spins through the air and phases right through him.

Leonidas sighs. "Kid, you can't hurt me, nor can I hurt you." Leonidas walks up to Carter and swings his arm through.

"You phase through me like a ghost." Carter's eyes are wide under the mask.

"A ghost is a good way to look at my being. I can touch and lift things in the world while also phasing through them all the same." Leonidas demonstrates with a piece of paper.

"But what's stopping you from hurting me?" Carter asks.

"If there is no Evil Alliance, then I am not active. And I prefer to be awake then asleep," Leonidas says.

Carter deactivates his armor and walks over to the table. "So why are you here?"

"I want to warn you of the fights that are to come."

"What fights?" Carter tilts his head like a dog.

"Carter, there are people who want your power. The fact that you somehow found the temple before some big corporation with professionals is crazy!"

"Well, it wasn't easy, and I didn't do much work. My father did. I just put the last few pieces together and got a few possible locations. It just so happens the second one I went to was it." Carter rubs the back of his head.

"Where was the first location?"

"A sewer."

"Oh, fun. Regardless, if people see any of you or your four other team members, I guarantee a few groups will mobilize and attempt to capture you. They'll try to learn as much as they can from you and then kill you."

"There are only three of us."

"Wait, what?!"

"Yeah, it's just me as Karma, my friend Jimena as Devil, and my friend Logan as Luck."

"Are you serious? You activated the temple with only three people inside?!" Leonidas shouts.

"We didn't expect the temple to activate, let alone give us powers!" Carter shouts back.

Leonidas rubs his forehead. "Okay. We can work with this. How much fighting experience do you have?"

"I'm a self-taught swordsman; I can dual wield swords."

"Well, it's a start. Try testing out your powers on people. Do some people watching and try to read into their karma. You don't have to act on them, but at least get a feel for it. Now then, I'll leave you to your own devices." Leonidas starts to walk away, then stops for a moment and turns to Carter. "One last thing. Don't let your powers consume you," Leonidas says then vanishes from sight.

"Well, Jimena, it doesn't look like I'll be able to lie low forever. We have some conflict on the horizon, and I have a feeling we won't be able to ignore it," Carter says to himself, looking out the window.

CHAPTER SEVEN

Carter's phone blares a noisy, annoying alarm. He rolls over in his bed with his eyes still closed as he smacks his phone, turning off the alarm.

"Get up, you fool. Just because you live alone doesn't mean I won't bug you," an unknown voice says while ripping the blanket off Carter, dressed in sleep shorts and a tank top. Carter's eyes burst open. He feels a jolt run through his body, telling him to fight, and without thinking, he leaps out of the bed and pounces on top of the other person, pinning them to the floor. He raises his fist, ready to swing when he sees Dawn's frightened face and flush red cheeks.

"Oh shit, Dawn! I-I didn't mean to!"

"It's fine. I shouldn't have woken you so abruptly. I know ever since the incident, you've been on high alert when you sleep." Dawn turns her gaze away from him.

"Hey, are you okay?" Carter asks, stepping closer to her.

"I'm fine, it's just … this wasn't how I expected to be pinned down by you," Dawn says quietly.

Carter looks at how they're positioned on the floor and scrambles off her. "Sorry about that," he says, helping Dawn to her feet.

"Carter, you're fine. It's my fault for not being considerate about how you would react. Now, hurry up and get ready. It's time for school." Dawn quickly leaves Carter's room and shuts the door. Minutes later, he comes out fully dressed, sporting a pair of jeans, a gray undershirt, and a lightweight red jacket with a lone black sleeve.

"Just so you know, I didn't give you a key to my house so you can wake me up in the morning," Carter says while adjusting his shirt. He walks to the kitchen to find Dawn making toast. "I also didn't give it to you so you can eat my food."

"I'm not making this for me. I'm making this for you."

"Well, my point still stands. You have plenty of food at your mansion and a father who loves the hell out of you. You know how many rich kids are just given money and nothing else?"

"For the last time, Carter, it's not a mansion, it is just a large house and I stay at the HQ because it's closer to school. And another thing, I don't associate myself with rich kids because they're snobby," Dawn says, putting apricot preserves on the two slices of warm toast. She sits next to Carter at the table and slides him the plate while he ties his shoes.

"Are you sure it's not because you grew up with me long before your dad's company took off, so you know what it's like to be friends with someone poor?" Carter asks. Dawn ignores the question and just stares at Carter as she fiddles with her hair. He then tries to say something to her but just makes muffled noises.

"Carter, finish eating before speaking. Also, hurry up. We don't wanna be late or Ms. Morris will be pissed at us—more you than me." Dawn gets up and goes into the garage. Carter quickly finishes his food and chugs a glass of water, dashes into the garage with his backpack in hand. Carter pulls out his keys and turns the ignition on his motorcycle. It fails to start, only making snapping noises.

"Dammit! Stupid piece of junk!" Carter says, kicking the bike.

"Hey, hey, hey! Calm down, we can walk. We won't have any free time before class, but we will at least be there on time." Dawn grabs his hands and pulls him away from the bike. The two begin their journey to school on foot, walking in silence for a while. "Are you excited to go back to school?" Dawn asks.

"Yep, super excited." Carter rolls his eyes.

"Poop head. Well, let's change the topic before we get to school. Oh yeah, I forgot to ask this the other day, but how did your search for the Evil Alliance temple go?"

Carter freezes for a second. "No luck. I was wrong; it wasn't there."

"Damn, really? You were so confident in your work. I remember when you figured it out while I was watching TV, you were so ecstatic and excited. I wish I could have gone, but my father needed me at home."

"I was really hoping to find it," Carter says, hoping she bought the bluff.

"That sucks. I wish it was there, then we could become the next generation. Then you can be Karma and I could be your loving Devil," Dawn says, clinging to his arm. "By the way, maybe you know the answer to this. So the five members are supposed to be aspects of misfortunes, or possible misfortunes. So what is the deal with Devil? Like, you have Karma, Luck, Curse, and Jinx, but what's with Devil? What makes it a misfortune?"

"Believe it or not, you're not the first person to ask that question. The working theory for Devil is that it's the concept of being dragged down to hell by the devil. Back in the day, when certain people would act oddly or unlike themselves, people would assume they were possessed by the devil and the devil was trying to drag them down to hell sooner than intended. These actions would frighten the people around them, who would then either burn them at the stake like witches or torture them with like holy water or something like that."

Dawn nods her head in response. "So Devil is more along the lines of possession and influence?"

"In a way, yes. The apparent powers of the five members are a working theory based on common knowledge and what has been observed by the previous generations. Since they are a group built on secrecy, it's hard to know exactly what their powers are. The Evil Alliance is centuries old. To know the point behind their creation is a mystery. For all we know, the powers are not based on what we know today and are actually completely different."

"Very interesting. You sure do know a lot about it. I mean, it's to be expected, coming from you," Dawn says with a smile as she gazes at Carter's face. "Anyway, are you gonna try dating again?"

"W-What? Why are you bringing that up?" Carter stammers, flinching at her question.

"Well, new school, new people, new single ladies. I guarantee there's at least ten girls looking for a six-foot-two man like yourself they want to climb up on." She gives Carter a nudge with her elbow. "But hey, I'm still here too. I would love to be in a deeper relationship with you."

"Stop talking about me being your boyfriend, okay? I said no already." Carter's face turns a faint red. "I want us to stay friends."

"I know, I know. I do really care about you, and you know my feelings. I also understand you feel you're still broken from your last relationship, but I just want you to know that I'm here and I will always be on your side," Dawn says with a smile.

"It's not that I haven't considered a relationship with you. I actually have, but I'm not ready for it." Carter sighs while looking into her eyes. Dawn gives him a bear hug.

"I appreciate your honesty, Carter. And when you feel like you're ready, I'll be waiting for you."

"Dawn, you shouldn't keep waiting for me, though. I don't know how long it could be until I'm ready, and if you want to have that kind of relationship with someone, you should. Preferably someone without the issues I have," Carter says, only to look to his side and find Dawn is missing. He turns around and sees Dawn standing still, clenching her fists.

"What makes you think you have the right to say that?" Dawn rushes over to Carter, getting in his face. "Carter, I have the right to choose who I want to be with! I love you for you! You are someone special. You're so caring and you've helped out so many people over the years I've known you, and-and-and you don't know how to ask for help. You're a hero to others, but you need someone to be your hero. That is something you will probably never understand, and that's fine. But I'll be damned if I don't try!" Dawn finishes her scolding, taking a deep breath. "Also, any boys who do try to talk to me only know me as the daughter of a rich CEO, so most of the time, they're out to get something. All right, we're almost there!" Her instant tone shift sends a shiver down Carter's spine.

After a few more minutes of talking, they arrive at Castle High School. The front entrance to the school looks like a drawbridge to match the multiple towers located through the school, which are used as stairwells.

"I still think it's a stupid name for a school," Carter tells Dawn.

"Oh, come on. It's not that bad." She nudges his side. The two spend some time walking around the school, passing doors and other students until they find a sign covered with classroom numbers and corresponding last names. Carter runs his finger along the sign.

"Dawn, we're in room four twenty-seven," he says. The two head up a flight of stairs to find the four hundred hall, then search for the correct room. Dawn bumps into another girl, who drops stuff on the floor.

"I'm so sorry! I wasn't paying attention to where I was going!" The girl quickly picks up her fallen items while pushing her long, straightened brown hair out of her face. Dawn helps her and the two make eye contact. They stare at each other for a minute. "Dawn?!"

"River, is that you?!" Dawn's eyes widen.

"It is you!" River squeals with glee and hugs Dawn, dropping all her stuff again. The two girls laugh in their embrace while Carter sighs and picks everything back up.

"Oh my god, how are you? It's been forever!" Dawn asks, separating from their hug.

"I've been doing well. You look good yourself. What about you? How are you doing?"

"Oh, you know, just hanging around day by day."

"Isn't your father's company doing really well? That doesn't make your life crazy?"

"No, actually. My father likes to keep me out of it to help me have as normal of a life I can."

"That's awesome. Oh yeah, did you ever get with Carter?" River looks at her.

"Why don't you ask him yourself?" Dawn looks over to Carter as he stands, River's things cradled in his arms.

"Oh, wow! You, um … You look big." River gets closer to Carter, inspecting him all over. The two lock eyes for a moment as Carter stares back into River's muddy yellow eyes above the faint freckles that run along her pale cheeks.

"Thanks?" Carter tilts his head.

"What I meant to say is that you're tall now, and very broad. Is that the right word? Regardless, you're not that short chubby kid anymore," River says with a smile, hiding her rose-tinted cheeks.

"I don't recall being chubby, and me and Dawn are not a thing."

"Regardless, you really filled out." River jabs his shoulder lightly. "Anyway, it was nice seeing you two. I hope we have a class together. Talk to you guys later." River takes back her items from Carter's arms. She turns, waves goodbye, and dashes away.

"Why did she say 'regardless' twice?" Carter raises a brow.

"Some things never change. Guess I have some competition, then." Dawn smirks.

"What's that supposed to mean?"

"I guess we should go to our homeroom too," Dawn says while heading in the opposite direction of River.

"Hey, what is it supposed to mean?" Carter follows Dawn while still looking in the direction River went. The first bell rings and the two quickly pick up the pace.

"Found it," Dawn says. They walk into a room that's nearly empty, save for seven other students in a room large enough for thirty or more kids. They go to a table and sit down. The final bell rings and the teacher rambles on about the new year and school rules. Minutes later, they pass out schedules to what few students there are.

Carter pulls out a piece of paper to write down his schedule, but he stops when he finds a note scribbled on the page.

Carter, be on your guard. Those who are searching for you and your friends are closer than you think. With your incident at the summer camp reaching the news, people are on the hunt for you now. Leonidas.

"Thanks for telling me," Carter says to himself, then looks up at Dawn. "If what he said is true, I have to make sure my friends don't get involved," Carter whispers, putting the paper away.

"Say something?" Dawn asks.

"Nope, just humming a song that's stuck in my head." Carter smiles and Dawn responds with a giggle. Homeroom ends and Carter heads to his first class. Upon entering the classroom, he hears someone call his name. He turns his gaze and sees River, waving her arm frantically. Carter sighs and sits next to her. "River, are you gonna be this obnoxious every day? 'Cause if that's the case, I don't want to sit next to you."

"No, it's just for today, I promise," she says, smirking.

"Good, 'cause I would like to focus in class and not have a wailing child trying to get my attention all the time." Carter pulls out a notebook and sets it down in front of him.

"So if you and Dawn are here, that means Logan and Jimena are here too, huh?"

"No, they're at a different school."

"What, really?! You four were inseparable. It's weird not seeing you guys together. Did something happen?"

"No, nothing … happened. Ms. Morris didn't feel comfortable with me going to a school further away from her, so she asked me to come here. She offered for everyone to come as well, but the other two preferred to stay there. I didn't have much say, as she is my guardian. And Dawn came with me to make sure I wasn't lonely."

"That's sweet. She's always there for you." River smiles then looks forward as the teacher begins talking.

A few hours later, Carter enters his fifth class for the day.

"Hello, Lola—I mean, Ms. Morris," Carter stutters.

"Hello, Carter. Welcome to World History. Take a seat," Lola

says in a stern tone. Carter turns his gaze and sees all the chairs

are in pairs of two at each small table. River and Dawn are talking

to each other at one table. He makes his way to a lone table in the

corner and waits for the lesson to start.

The bell rings and Lola heads to the front of the room.

"Hello, class. I hope your first day today has gone well so far. I see

some familiar faces and some new ones. For those who don't

know, I am Ms. Morris, and I will be your World History teacher

this year. I'm also the head of the history department, so if you

have any questions regarding history, I'll gladly help you out." Lola

smiles and continues with the class, going over routines and what

the year will be like.

Lola Morris

Chapter Eight

Carter zones out for the rest of the day, only thinking about what Leonidas said to him. The hours pass by, and eventually, Carter and Dawn regroup to go home.

"Carter, you've been very quiet today. Even in Ms. Morris' class, you didn't say anything. Is everything okay?" Dawn grabs his hand.

"I'm fine, I just … I feel like I missed the temple when I searched for it," Carter lies.

"What do you mean? I thought you didn't find it?" Dawn tilts her head.

"I didn't, but I feel like I didn't search everywhere I could have. And I guess it's just been in the back of my mind, bothering me."

"Oh, I'm sorry. I didn't realize it was bothering you so much." Dawn hugs Carter, and a car pulls up in front of the two. The window rolls down and Mr. Shardlow appears behind it, smiling. "Dad, why do you have a ridiculous look on your face?"

"Oh, is it not funny? I was hoping it would be funny. Well, I'm here to pick you up so we can get to our appointment," he says, unlocking the door.

"Oh, right." Dawn climbs into the car.

"Sorry, Carter, I would like to give you a ride, but you would be stuck with us for a few boring hours."

"It's okay, I don't live all that far away," Carter says.

"Get home safe, Carter. I'll see you tomorrow." Dawn waves goodbye as the two drive off.

"Today went by fast. I sure hope every day is like this," Carter says to himself. He comes up to an alley, and a shiver runs through him. A feeling of danger pulses within. "Do some practicing with my powers, huh? All right, then. Let's do just that."

Carter smirks and walks down the alley, transforming halfway and

stopping in the center of an open area. He spins around for a

moment, looking at all the garbage and discarded furniture. He

closes his eyes for a moment and takes a deep breath. Focusing

his mind, he tries to picture a radar sensor in his mind. After a

moment, a red dot appears behind him on his mental radar. He

opens his eyes and turns to face it. "I know you're there, so don't

bother hiding," Carter says, and soon, the rustle of trash bags and

cans fill the alley. A few men carrying bats and knives emerge,

smiling at Carter. His eyes widen under the mask; he wasn't

expecting so many people.

"You're a pretty cocky kid to come into our territory and

demand we come out," one of them says with a grin.

"Tell your friends to stop hiding, too." Carter watches as

more members of the group file out.

"Well now, kid, how about you give us all your valuables and we won't hurt you?" a man who's better dressed asks, stepping forward.

"Not a chance," Carter says with a smile.

"Who do you think you are? No matter. Get 'im, boys."

Carter holds up his fists, ready to fight. Right as he's about to move, he sneezes. "Ugh, gross." He takes the bottom part of his mask off and wipes it on his coat. "I hope this coat doesn't stain." He slips his mask back on and then spins around, kicking one of the men trying to catch Carter off guard. One by one, they approach Carter in an attempt to subdue him. Carter keeps up with most of them, dodging the majority of the attacks, with a few getting through and knocking him backward. He fights back, launching heavy punches back at them.

As he fights, one of the men bashes Carter with their body, pushing him into someone else. The goon wraps his arm around

Carter's throat, trying to hold him still. One of the guys rushes in and swings their fist at Carter's chest. They scream out in pain after hitting the metal plate of his armor. Carter breaks free of the headlock and throws the subduer into the wall, but soon after, he's tackled from the side, landing in stray trash cans. The attacker grabs one of the cans and bashes it into Carter a few times. He catches the can in his hand, looks down, and sees the attacker's leg. He kicks their knee, causing them to kneel; Carter kicks him in the face, then hops to his feet and kicks the can away. He turns to the remaining people. They begin to shuffle backward, receding into the corners of the alley.

"Where's all that smack talk from earlier, huh?" Carter spins around, his arms wide. He closes his eyes for a moment and thinks about using his powers more. "The powers of Karma are about equality and fairness. Equal Vision is what allows me to see it," Carter whispers to himself.

One of the goons, armed with a bat, charges toward him, swinging furiously. Carter turns and catches the bat in his hand. His vision loses color and highlighted points appear over the goon's body, including their face. Carter focuses on their now terrified face and is sent a vision of them beating up another person with the bat. He sees them smash the person's face in, brutally crushing their skull and continuing even after their death. Carter's vision returns to normal and he rips the bat out of the goon's hand. He flips the bat so the handle is in his hand, then swings it across their face. The goon falls to the ground and Carter smashes the bat into their skull, exacting the same trauma they gave others.

After a moment, Carter stands up straight with the blood-covered bat in his hand. The rest of the group immediately runs away, pushing past their leader, who gets frightened and attempts to flee, but trips and falls on the ground. A gun slides out from him. He reaches out and grabs it, turns back to Carter, then shoots. Carter draws his sword and quickly smacks the bullet out of the way. He walks over to the leader and kicks the gun out of his hand, then picks him up by the collar with one hand.

"I'm sorry; I'm just trying to make money to support my family!"

"It's called a job. Attacking people will get you nowhere." Carter begins to see red highlighted parts on his body, one on the left leg, one on his right lung, and one on his head, all with their own visions of heinous acts committed against someone else. "You take a life, you gotta pay for it."

"No, please! I'll give you whatever you want, please!"

Carter ignores the man's pleas as he takes his sword and swiftly thrusts it through the man's head. "You get what you deserve." Carter drops the man, his body smacking onto the cold pavement, leaving a splatter of blood around his head. Carter lowers his blade as blood drips from the tip onto the ground. He takes a deep breath and gives the sword a swing, ridding it of most of the blood. He steps over the unconscious bodies and into the light of the afternoon sun. His legs become uneasy, and he breathes heavily for a moment as he slumps against a wall. "I just killed two people."

"It won't be the last time, either."

Carter whips around to see Leonidas standing there. "Is this your whole shtick? You just appear to give nonsense advice and then peace out? 'Cause I'm telling you now, it'll get annoying real quick."

"You saw it, didn't you? You saw your Equal Vision? If someone harmed or killed someone, you can see exactly how and where, so you can deliver that same pain. You had three options: two leading to death, one leading to a severed leg. Why the head?" Leonidas asks.

"I don't need you to explain my own powers to me, Leonidas. I'm not a child."

"Can you just answer the question?!"

"Fine!" Carter looks down at his hands, clenching his fists. He looks back up to Leonidas. "I saw … I saw him kill a little girl, not much older than five. He shot her right in the head. She was terrified, sitting in between her two parents in their own pools of blood. He looked that girl in the eyes and smiled like what he was doing was fun. When I saw that, I knew he deserved to die." Carter clenches his fists tighter.

"Carter, you will need to get over these things or else every time you see those visions, you'll get emotional and make choices based on emotion rather than reason."

"I understand that, but it's just …" Carter slams his fist against the wall. "Fine, I'll do my best to not let my emotions dictate my actions." Carter takes a deep breath and deactivates his armor, then resumes his journey home.

Later, Carter questions himself. "What have I done?" Thoughts flood his mind constantly, rattling his thoughts, trying to determine right from wrong. He does chores in silence, replaying what happened earlier. His phone ringing interrupts his thoughts—Jimena. He swipes his finger across the screen. "Hello?"

"Carter, if you can hear me, I need help. There's too many of them!" a voice shouts, followed by loud bangs.

"Where are you?!" Carter asks urgently.

"I'm at Parabi Park. There's some anti-vigilante organization or something after me. Please hurry!"

"I'm on my way!" Carter says, darting to the garage and trying to start up his bike again. "Come on, you damn thing! Work!" Carter smacks the bike, and as he does so, the color of the bike changes to a black and red design. Leonidas appears in front of Carter.

"Congrats on finding another form of your power. Karma's Curse. Turn anything into something useful for a short time. And Carter, be careful. These are the guys who want to use your powers. They have weapons that can seriously harm you."

"Noted." Carter smiles, and the motorcycle roars to life.

Chapter Nine

"I have to hurry or Jimena might get hurt!" Carter says, running a red light and causing two cars to swerve nearly hitting each other. He drives quickly through the city until he reaches the park. Carter swiftly turns, causing his bike to slide as he jumps off, landing in front of the park entrance as he delves deep into it. The ground shakes him to his knees, and a loud bang created from a cloud of fire and smoke sounds. "Oh god, please let Jimena be okay!" Several people are dressed in dark black onesies covered in maroon metallic armor with their left arms covered with a large gauntlet covering rifles firing red lasers.

"This park looks like a warzone." Another explosion occurs. "Are they dropping bombs?!" Carter looks in their direction of fire and sees Jimena hiding behind a large rock that has mostly been blown away from the raining fire. *There she is! That rock won't hold for much longer*. Carter draws his swords and begins his charge onto the battlefield.

One of the grunts turn and sees Carter dashing toward them. "Karma is on the field—" Carter slices their throat before they can finish speaking. Most of the grunts turn toward Carter and fire their rifles. He tries to side step to avoid the majority of the blasts. He swings his sword to cut the laser, splitting a bullet in two, causing the bolt to hit him and the other part to fly past. Step by step, he's hit as he continues his mad dash, cutting down those who face him. Each swing of his blade takes down a target in an instant, cutting through their armor like scissors gliding through paper. Carter doesn't stop until he reaches Jimena and takes a seat right next to her. He takes a few deep breaths, assessing his wounds.

"So what was that about staying out of the way and lying low?" Carter asks.

"Really? That's the first thing you say to me in this situation!"

"Yeah, it is. So how was your first day at school?" Carter asks with a straight face. Jimena sighs and turns her gaze toward the battlefield.

"Not bad until now, yours?" Jimena asks, trying to focus on the battle.

"Okay. I killed some punks in an alley and some peeps trying to get to you."

"Oh, okay. Sounds good… Wait, what? You *killed* someone?!"

"Yep, and I'm about to do it again to save your ass," he says, then vaults over the rock. He doesn't even make it over when he gets blasted in the chest and thrown back onto the ground next to Jimena. "Oh, that hurt."

"Was that your attempt at being cool? 'Cause if it was, I can assure you it was not."

"Ha, ha. Very funny," Carter says as he sits up.

"Logan is on his way, but now that you're here, I can try this out on a large group of people." Jimena slams her pitchfork into the ground. The tips begin to light up, along with the ground surrounding it. Carter turns his head around the corner of the rock and sees the closest guards locked in place, shaking as if they're being electrocuted.

"Someone's been playing with their powers." Carter smiles and dashes out from behind the rock, dodging the few lasers shot by the smaller group of grunts out of Jimena's range. He takes down those who are locked in place and then makes his way up to the others. Carter freezes as several trucks pull into a parking lot and unload dozens of gunmen.

"Oh, crap. That's not good. We need to get out of here!" Carter turns and sees more gunmen and what looks like a tank from the future roll into the park. The tank fires a giant laser at the rock Jimena is hiding behind and it destroys it, revealing her. *I need to stop that thing before it fires again.* Carter runs toward it. The tank wastes no time, turning toward Carter and blasting him, sending him flying across the park and slamming into a tree. He tries to stand up, but slides back down the tree. "Damn, that hurt really bad. If I didn't have these powers, I'd probably be dead."

"All soldiers attack Devil. I will handle Karma," a robotic voice says. Carter balks as everyone turns their aim toward Jimena, preparing to unleash their attacks.

"Get up, you thief, and face me." The voice comes from a person covered in armor, carrying a Katana with a red blade. The person points their blade at him. Carter uses his swords to help him stand up, griping both swords tightly.

"How can we face each other if we're both wearing masks?" Carter asks sarcastically.

"What? Are you mocking me?!"

"Aww, do you not like being mocked? I can provide a sarcastic comment if you'd like?"

"Shut your mouth! You will die by my hand and I shall claim your power for our grand plan!" the robotic soldier shouts.

"How about this? I'll put one sword away, so it's fair," Carter says as he slides one sword back into place.

"It won't matter. You will fall by my hand regardless of how many blades you have!" The two get ready to duel, while Jimena fends off the gunmen as best she can.

"Well, you fell for my distraction," Carter says.

"What distraction?"

Carter smiles under his mask. "You let me stall long enough to heal up." Carter looks over at Jimena. "Please, Logan, get here soon," Carter whispers to himself as he turns back to the soldier. "Let's get to work, shall we?" Carter lunges forward, initiating the fight.

The gunmen approach Jimena. They begin taking turns shooting lasers at her. Jimena steps side to side avoiding the lasers like a spy sneaking around. She throws her pitchfork into the ground as it locks more people in place. Jimena rushes forward and rips her weapon out of the ground and smacks them across the head knocking most of them out or at least stunning them. As she leaps high in the air to avoid a tank blast she gets shot in the air and falls to the ground. She holds her wound as she struggles to get up.

The two swordsman's blades clash immediately, constantly smacking against each other, blocking and deflecting each other's strikes. Both are unable to land a single blow on the other. Carter slams the ground with his sword and jumps over the soldier, leaving the sword in the ground. As he jumps, he flips over and draws the other sword, slicing the soldier in their back. The soldier trembles, regains balance, then faces Carter again.

"Aww, what's wrong? Don't like that I didn't play fair? You were the one who said you could take me down regardless of how many blades I use."

"You annoying little brat!" they shout.

Carter chuckles in response. "So, what's your name?"

"My name is Titan."

"Okay, Titan. Firstly, your swordsmanship is quite terrible. Secondly, aren't titans supposed to be threatening? I ain't scared of you!" Titan clicks their tongue and raises their arm. A tank changes its aim from Carter to Jimena and fires.

"No!" Carter screams as Jimena's body is engulfed by the flames of an explosion. He falls onto his knees, his hands shaking violently. He breathes rapidly, clenching his fists. Suddenly, all the color from Carter's coat vanishes until it's all black. A different tank fires a shot at him. He stands up and sticks out his hand to the laser shot at him by the tank. The laser stops at his hand and begins to shrink as the energy from the laser transfers into his armor, reigniting the color in his coat and making it glow brighter. He screams out in pain for a moment, only to stop in place as he feels himself being stabbed.

"Cheap shot," Carter says. His aura radiates energy and pushes Titan off him, leaving the sword still wedged in his back. Carter grabs the blade, pulls it out, and looks over to Jimena to see her body on the ground, battered and bruised. Titan gets up and rushes over to Carter. He doesn't hesitate and moves faster than normal, appearing behind Titan with his sword in one hand and Titan's sword in the other. He swings a sword swiftly, slicing into Titan's left leg. *Damn, this blade isn't sharp enough.* Carter turns to Titan and kicks them over to a tree, then throws the

Katana at him, staking them to the tree in the stomach. He then makes one long jump to the tank. Carter lifts his blade and stabs it into the tank, then runs back and forth on top of it, tearing the tank up.

"Help me," says Jimena in a faint voice. He turns and sees Jimena reaching out to him. Carter runs over to her as he sees another tank pull onto the battlefield and fire at her. The explosion coats the area in flames.

"No!" Carter yells, walking slowly toward the explosion. "No, no, no— What?" He squints his eyes, seeing a bubble being born from the flames.

"Sorry for the late arrival!" Logan says. He stands inside the bubble, holding up his axe. "Carter, go get them. I'll take care of Jimena."

"Thanks, Logan. Now, who wants to die?" A horde of soldiers point their guns at Carter. His coat goes back to normal as he readies his blades. He wastes no time disposing of the remaining enemies until there are none left but the lone second tank. Carter is about to attack it when Logan flies over Carter and smashes his axe into it, tearing it up with hefty swings, ripping open the tank walls in a matter of seconds.

Carter turns around and sees Titan rushing over to him with their sword in hand. "Ready for round two, Titan? En garde!" Their blades clash against each other, bouncing away, only to be brought back and swung once again. Titan slows down, and all of their attacks are countered by Carter, resulting in multiple wounds from Carter's swords. "What's wrong? Can't keep up?" He swings harder, knocking Titan's sword from their hand, then quickly ducks and swings his leg, tripping Titan. Carter gets to his feet and points his sword at Titan's neck. They lie defenseless, and Carter angles his blade to pierce right through their heart. "Now you will … Never mind." Carter puts his swords away and reaches down to

Titan's side, ripping off an empty sheath. Titan tries to reach for it, their arm shaking. Carter walks away with it over to where the red Katana landed, then slides it into the sheath. He turns to look at Titan as Logan appears behind him, carrying Jimena in his arms. "Leave."

"You think you can just insult me, take my weapon, and expect me to leave? No way, buddy," Titan says while trying to sit up. They raise their arm and quickly disappear. Carter turns to the side and sees Titan dangling from a rope attached to a small helicopter, flying away.

"I just told them to leave, they said no, and now they're leaving?" Carter tilts his head at Logan, who shrugs his shoulders. Carter holds out his hand, which begins to glow as a black and red pistol forms. He pulls the trigger, firing a magic bullet that pierces the air, leaving behind a red muzzle flash and a whistle. The helicopter rocks a little before disappearing from their sight.

"Damn, they got away. You really almost had them," Logan says, looking toward the sky.

"Thanks for your input, Logan." The gun in Carter's hand vanishes. His vision locks onto a piece of metal that was stripped from the tank off in the distance. "What's that?"

"What's what?" Logan turns to Carter.

Carter picks up the piece and looks at the branding painted on it. "It says Iron Organization." Carter places his other hand on the piece and closes his eyes. Images flash in his mind, showing the factory where the tank was made, surrounded by scientists and engineers testing the lethality of the tanks blasts against live subjects.

"Carter!" Logan yells. Carter turns around as the images fade away and he walks over to Logan. "Jimena's hurt badly. Why isn't she healing?"

"I could ask the same thing myself," Carter says. "Let's get back to my place. I know someone who can help." Logan tilts his head in confusion. "I'll explain later. Let's just go to my place, okay? It's the closest. Also, I don't think Jimena's mom would like to see her all beat up like this." The two take off to Carter's motorcycle while carrying Jimena.

Dawn Shardlow

Chapter Ten

They ride off back to Carter's home, arriving in only a few minutes. Both Logan and Carter deactivate their armor. Carter opens the doors and the two enter, Logan carrying Jimena over to a couch and setting her down. Logan looks up and sees Leonidas sitting at the table, reading through papers.

"Who are you?!" Logan yells.

"Leonidas, don't you have anything better to do?" Carter asks.

"No, I don't, actually," Leonidas says. "What happened to her?"

"You were right, Leonidas. It was that group you warned me about."

"Wait, I'm confused. Who is he, and why are you telling him these things?" Logan asks in a panic.

"He's the spirit of the Evil Alliance and is basically a ghost, so we can't do much about him," Carter says, quickly catching Logan up.

"How do we remove her armor?" Logan asks while looking at Leonidas.

"She has to do it herself," Leonidas says. "It's a built-in protection system for both the user's health and their identities. So we wait until she wakes up and deactivates it herself. In the meantime, let's talk about what happened out there tonight." Leonidas clears the table. Logan throws a blanket on top of Jimena and joins Leonidas. Carter grabs a chair and sits down at the table, holding his hand over his stab wound as it heals slower than normal.

"So what do we know?" Leonidas asks.

Carter takes the Katana strapped to his side off and sets it on the table. "I got that from their leader. They go by Titan." Carter pulls the sword out of its sheath, the red blade shining in the light.

Logan picks up the blade and inspects it. "They call themselves the

Iron Organization. What they want with our powers, I don't know,

but Titan did call me a thief."

"Well, that's not much to go off of," Leonidas says.

"Hold on." Carter holds his free arm up. "When I touched

one of the broken pieces of the tank, I got one of those visions you

told me about. But it wasn't the first time I felt that one

specifically."

"Where did you feel it before?" Logan asks, setting down

the sword. Carter goes over to his school bag, pulls something out,

and sets it on the table.

"A metal brick?" Leonidas asks, looking at it. Carter grabs it

again and shakes it, creating the helmet that was given to him. "A

helmet?"

"No, what's under the helmet—yes, the helmet!" Carter takes it and flips it over, showing the Iron Works branding.

"Oh, okay. Who is Iron Works?" Leonidas asks. Carter shrugs. "So you knew they were the ones after us, but you don't know who they are?!" Carter clenches his fists, his eye twitching.

"Look, I took a guess, based on the fact that not many people can go toe to toe with one of you. I figured Jimena was fighting someone with Rood Staal weapons." Leonidas rubs his neck.

"Did you forget none of us have proper combat training?!" Carter says.

Logan looks at the sword. "Wait, rude stall weapons?"

Leonidas turns toward him. "Rood Staal. It's Dutch for red steel. Rood Staal has the ability to nullify magic temporarily. That's why getting hit by something once or twice with this isn't gonna kill you right away."

"Well, they have a plethora of effective weaponry at their disposal, including tanks!"

"Damn, things have really gotten worse since the last Evil Alliance," Leonidas whispers to himself.

"But what would Iron Works want from the Evil Alliance?" Logan asks, checking on Jimena.

Carter rests his fist on his chin. "I don't know, but I can get an inside look."

"How are you going to do that?" Leonidas asks.

"Carter is best friends with the CEO's daughter, Dawn," Logan says.

"Carter, if you pry into the company, you need to be very careful. Do you know if she's wrapped up in this at all?"

"I'm not sure. She has expressed interest in the Evil Alliance, but that was only because I was interested in it. I'm in pretty good standing with her father, and he's made me many offers. I'm sure being able to take a tour of the facility wouldn't be too hard to get."

"Guys, she's waking up!" Logan shouts. Carter and Leonidas rush over to Jimena's side.

She opens her eyes slowly, then touches her face, still feeling the mask. "Ugh, what happened?" Jimena turns and looks at everyone.

"We'll explain in a second, but for now, deactivate your armor," Carter says.

Jimena takes a deep breath, and her armor disappears. "Did we win?"

Logan chuckles. "Yeah, we did."

"What do we do now?" she asks the three.

"Hey, how come she's not freaking out about me knowing who she is?" Leonidas asks.

Jimena smiles. "'Cause if these two are okay with you seeing me in my armor, I figured they have a good reason."

"She's the smartest out of us three," Carter says. Leonidas nods in response.

"Basically, for now, we're just gonna lie low while Carter charms his girlfriend to get to her dad's company as they are the ones who attacked us," Logan says, giving her the rundown.

"Dawn is not my girlfriend!" Carter shouts. "But yes, Iron Works is connected to the so-called Iron Organization, and now that I say them both out loud, it feels a little too obvious and really dumb to call your villainous operation a slight variation of your own company's name." Carter turns to Leonidas. "So, Mister Knows Everything, what's our next move?"

"For now, stay as hidden as possible. Help where you can, and if the Iron Organization starts to follow you, lose them or dispose of them," Leonidas says. "I need to go. Good luck."

Leonidas vanishes.

"So, what's his deal? Is he some wizard or something?" Jimena asks the two.

"Leonidas is the spirit of the Evil Alliance. His job is to act as a guide to us. Although, from what I have read, he doesn't appear for every generation. He was made out to be a myth, or a simple illusion that gives wisdom. Not even my father's research mentions his appearance, let alone him having a name," Carter says. He picks up the sword and notices a small box attached to the side of the sheath. He opens it up, revealing cleaning supplies. He sits down and cleans up the blade, then slides it back into the sheath. Carter holds it in his hand and tightens his grip on it, then closes his eyes.

"Uh, Carter, what are you doing?" Jimena asks.

"One of the powers I have is the ability to look into someone's or something's karma, almost like looking at events it has witnessed. The range of what I can see is short, but it gives me some hints. The more I do it, the better I will be at it, and possibly the more I could see," Carter says, taking a deep breath and trying to look into the sword's karma. He gets a few flashes of Titan brutally striking people down with that very sword. Carter jerks his head to the side, chills running down his spine, leaving goosebumps as he escapes the visions.

"Learn anything?" Logan asks.

"Only that Titan is a brutal killer and that I'm amazed we got out of that fight alive. But that means I should be able to find them easily if they have that much blood on their hands," Carter says, putting the sword away into a closet.

"Dude, it's eleven fifty-two. Should we go home?" Logan asks Carter.

"No, don't. We don't know what they're capable of, so let's stay low for a bit. Stay here. There are rooms you guys can use." Carter and Logan help Jimena to one of the beds and lie her down. Logan goes off to another bedroom for the night. Carter cleans up the living room to ensure there's no evidence. After a few minutes, he decides to go to bed but hears a knock at the door. His eyes widen with terror. "Did they find us already?" Carter walks over to the door, knife in hand. They knock again. He looks through the peephole but sees nothing. He quickly unlocks the door and raises the knife.

"Whoa, whoa, Carter! it's just me!" Dawn shouts. She stands in the doorway, dressed in loungewear, like she's ready for bed.

"Dawn, what the hell are you doing here this late at night?"

"Well … I kinda had a bad dream and couldn't go back to sleep. I know when I'm around you, I feel comfortable and warm, so I was wondering if I could spend the night."

"Dawn, it's tomorrow. Why did your dad even let you go out this late? How'd you even get here?" Carter sticks his head out and sees Dawn's family car drive away. "Goddammit, fine. Just go sleep on one of the guest beds." Carter turns around and sees Dawn is gone. He rushes inside and tries to look for her. He goes to the room where Jimena is and sees Dawn standing next to her. "Dawn, before you say anything."

Dawn turns to Carter, her face leaking tears. "What happened to her? Why is she here?" Dawn walks toward him. Carter grabs her hand and pulls her out of the room, then shuts the door. "Did you do that to her?"

"No, I didn't." Carter opens another door to show Logan passed out on a bed. "Jimena's neighborhood got attacked, and she got caught up in the crossfire. Me and Logan brought her here and made sure she was okay."

"Why didn't you take her to the hospital?"

"We … I don't have an answer for that."

"Stop standing there and let's take her!" Dawn walks back to her room, but stops when Carter grabs her hand.

"We can't."

"Why? Why can't we take one of your best friends to get help at a hospital?"

"She … doesn't have insurance, so she won't be able to pay for it," Carter says, blocking her path.

"Carter, did you forget you're friends with a millionaire? My father would have no problem paying for a hospital bill." Dawn smiles, placing her hand on Carter's face. He leans his face into her hand. Dawn's eyes widen in response.

"Dawn, this is more complicated than just her and her family. It was her choice to not go. I … I was just trying to help." Carter looks away.

"It's okay, Carter. I know you guys are all really close and you don't want to lose your friends. You won't. If you trust them, they will do what's right. And if she said she'll be fine, then I believe her. But if you feel things get worse, please let me know, okay?" Dawn stands on her tiptoes and kisses Carter's cheek. "I'll go sleep on the couch. You look exhausted; get some sleep. We still have class in the morning. Goodnight, Carter."

"You can come sleep with me … I don't think my couch is very comfy." Carter fidgets with his hands. Dawn smiles and joins Carter in his bedroom. The two get under the covers, Dawn lying next to him, but Carter facing away. Dawn shifts around until she is comfortable. A few minutes later, Carter's arms wrap around her and he lays his head on her chest, fast asleep. Dawn's face burns red as she rubs his head.

"You big ol' softy. You may act tough, but you're just as scared as the rest of us. Even someone like you needs to be protected once in a while." Dawn kisses his head before drifting off to sleep herself.

Carter opens his eyes to the bright light of the sun and an empty bed. He rubs his head. He gets dressed for the day, then leaves his room to check on Jimena, but she's not there. Carter turns to his head where his nose is leading him with the smell of bacon and eggs. He follows the smell and comes to find Dawn in the kitchen with an apron draped over her.

"Morning, Dawn."

"Morning, Carter. How'd you sleep last night?"

"I, uh … I slept fine, thank you. What about you?"

"To be honest, it was hard to get out of bed to call for rides to take Logan and Jimena home, but I managed." Dawn dishes up a plate and sets it on the table. "Hey, so my father invited you to some company party on Saturday. He wants to introduce you around, hoping you may be interested in one of the jobs there along with a general show around the Iron Works headquarters." Carter looks at Dawn as she pours him a glass of milk, then sets it in front of him.

Carter's mind races with all he could possibly uncover if he goes. "I would love to go!" Dawn smiles. "Oh, crap. I forgot I was going to have dinner with Lola that night." Carter scratches his head.

"I'm sure my father wouldn't mind inviting Ms. Morris," Dawn says.

"Then I'll let her know and we'll be all good to go!" Carter smirks at Dawn. She giggles and eats some food. The two chat and make their way to school to enjoy the rest of their day.

Chapter Eleven

Leonidas stands at Carter's kitchen table looking at papers illuminated by the lone light above, while Logan and Jimena sit on Carter's couch and watch TV. Carter comes out from his bedroom wearing a pair of red pants, a white undershirt, and an unbuttoned black dress shirt over it with the sleeves rolled up.

"Hey, guys, what looks better? Glasses or no glasses?" Carter asks.

"Carter, this is a mission, not a fun gathering. But I do have to say no glasses, as you haven't worn them in a while and it would be weird if you started to wear them again," Logan says.

"Logan is right; no glasses." Leonidas turns to him. "Also, this is a very important mission. You have the ultimate pass in, and the fact that it was just handed to you is kinda convenient. I would rather you get as much information now before you have to ask to be welcomed back, because if you were to get a job there, you would be confined to one area."

"Also, it would put you at a higher risk," Jimena adds.

"Yeah, yeah, yeah. I got it." Carter places his glasses on the counter.

"So let's run through the plan again. You're not going to do any fighting, just sneak around and gather as much intel as you can without getting in trouble." Leonidas picks up a paper and passes it to Carter. "This is a list of the general stuff that would be good to know, but your primary goal is to confirm that the two groups are in fact connected and their names aren't just a coincidence."

"Seems simple enough." Carter folds the list and puts it in his pocket.

"It may seem simple, but you know how complex they can be. Their technology is pretty advanced. Just look at that helmet he gave you. It folds up so nicely," Logan says. A car horn blares outside, followed by a muffled shout. Carter walks over to the front door and opens it to see Lola in her car.

"Come on, Carter. We don't want to be late!" Lola shouts excitedly from the car window.

"One sec, Lola!" Carter says, turning back inside.

"You got this, Carter. We'll be here, waiting for your information." Jimena holds up a notepad and pen. Carter nods and walks out the door to the car, adjusting his clothes. He gets in the car and turns to Lola.

"Aren't you excited?!" Lola has a big smile on her face.

Carter smirks, looking at Lola. "I am, but if you keep having that face, I might get too scared to go."

"I'm sorry, I just can't wait. Mr. Shardlow told me all about the great food that'll be there! Platters of rich and juicy meat! Exotic seafood from around the world! Do you know how much crab I can eat for *free?* I can imagine it now." Lola's mouth begins

to drool at the thought of the food.

"Okay, less drooling and more driving." Carter pats her

shoulder. The two drive off, making their way through the city,

arriving at the party in no time at all. Carter gets out of the car

and his eyes ascend the tall corporate building in front of them.

Lola goes over to Carter and wraps her arm around his.

"Onward, Carter! That food isn't gonna eat itself!" Lola

says. Carter sighs and the two walk to the doors, the

establishment looming larger with every step. Carter looks

around, noticing the overabundance of guards monitoring

everyone's move. As the two get closer, security increases and

more people queue to get in. The two step into the line and wait

as they move one group at a time, with many of the groups being

rejected for not being on the list and security forcing them out of

the way.

"Serves those phonies right. Not just anyone can get into this party; only those of the highest standard can get in," an older man dressed well in front of the two says as he watches security escort a couple out. The man moves to the front and is asked his name. "I am Mister Tempti. I'm on the list, don't worry."

"Sorry, there's no Tempti on here. Can I have your first name to search that way in case they put it down wrong?" the bouncer asks nicely, holding a capped pen, prepared to comb through the list.

"This is outrageous. I have been coming to Mr. Shardlow's business parties for years! I know the man very well. Look, he's right there. Mr. Shardlow! Over here!" Out from the shadows of the doorway, Mr. Shardlow appears.

"What's the problem here?"

"It's nice to see you, Mr. Shardlow. This incompetent bouncer of yours can't find my name on your list when I told him I was," Mr. Tempti says. The bouncer hands the list to Mr. Shardlow.

"Well, for one, Mr. Tempti, my bouncer is not incompetent—you are closer to that description. Apparently, you ignored the fact that you did not receive an invitation to my business party and assumed you could just come to my establishment to berate my employees and cause a scene in front of the doorway." Mr. Shardlow hands the list back to the bouncer and steps closer to Mr. Tempti. "The reason I didn't invite you to this party is because the business discussed at tonight's arrangement does not concern our partnership or any deals that would affect mine or your company, but clearly, you think this was all for you. And now that you've shown your gross bitterness and how you treat the average person, I have an inclination to sever our partnership. Your company is all for helping the less fortunate, but clearly, you have no respect for those kinds of people. Your greed for profit has clearly blinded you, Mr. Tempti." Mr. Shardlow looks to his left and sees Carter's shocked face. He stands up straight and brushes past Mr. Tempti. "Carter! Lola! So glad you guys could make it. Come on in, let me show you around!" Mr. Shardlow takes the two and brings them inside.

"Darson, you coward, get back here now!" Mr. Tempti shouts.

Mr. Shardlow stops. "One moment, you two." He goes back to the door and looks at Mr. Tempti. "We are done here, Mr. Tempti. I am withdrawing from our partnership. Actually, I have a better idea. I would recommend you downsize your luxury mansion. Have a good night. Security, if you would be so kind as to show Mr. Tempti his way out." Mr. Shardlow walks away while security drags Mr. Tempti out. Mr. Shardlow pulls out his phone, makes a call, then hangs up. He returns to the two and wraps his arms around their shoulders. "Sorry about that, you guys. Now then, where were we?"

He leads the two into what looks like the lobby of a large hotel adorned with beautiful art and plants. The main floor is decorated with tables and name plates placed in front of matching chairs. They all sit in front of a large stage placed at the end of the lobby. On either side, there are two glass elevator shafts with a solid stone base that lead up to the many floors full of offices and workshops. "Do you guys like the place? It used to be a hotel. After its closure, it was scheduled for demolition, but I swooped in, bought the place, and turned it into our headquarters." Mr. Shardlow praises his work as he walks them through the scenery. "Lola, I know you were excited about the food, but I have a confession to make."

"No, no, no. Please don't tell me there's not gonna be all of that good food?!" Lola grabs his hands, almost shedding a tear.

"I'm sorry, Lola, but there's even more food than I promised!" Mr. Shardlow turns her around to see a doorway at the edge of the room that leads to a ballroom filled with food. Her mouth opens wide as she slowly walks in.

"I, um … Carter, you have fun. I … I'm going to be in here, enjoying myself." Lola dashes in, giggling the entire time. Carter chuckles as he walks over to the edge of the tables. Most of the guests are already in their spots, with a few stragglers coming through the door and others leaving the room of food. Carter feels a tap on his shoulder. He turns around fast, extending his arm out and grabbing the person behind him. Mr. Shardlow holds his arms up.

"Whoa, sorry! I didn't mean to scare you that much," he says with a worried expression.

"I'm sorry, it's not you. A lot has happened recently and I—"

"Carter, you're okay. Dawn told me what happened to Jimena. How is she holding up, by the way?"

"She's doing better. A little shaken still, but other than that, okay," Carter says, taking a deep breath.

"That's good to hear. I know everything has been rough for you recently." Mr. Shardlow pats Carter's shoulder.

To change the subject, Carter raises a question. "Hey, what did you do with that grouchy business man? I saw you make a call after threatening him." Carter raises a brow.

Mr. Shardlow chuckles. "I bought his company. He and I formed a partnership years ago when my company wasn't as far along as it is today. We had both agreed to help each of our companies grow, but he sadly didn't provide the results he likes to think he did. I was thinking of ending things with him, but his company would serve better use under my wing rather than falling apart entirely. Now, enough rambling about business. Dawn isn't finished getting ready yet." Mr. Shardlow looks around and calls over one of his employees. "Please escort Mr. Shadson up to my daughter's room."

"Right away, sir."

"Encourage her to speed it up. Now then, I must greet more of my guests. Please excuse me, Carter," Mr. Shardlow says, then walks away.

"This way, Mr. Shadson." The guard leads the way, Carter following in tow. They step onto an elevator and rise several stories. As they ascend, Carter sends a text to Jimena about what he's noticed so far. He looks out the window in the elevator to see the party down below and realizes the lobby looks larger than it seems down there. At the top, the two step out and make their way down the hallway to stop at a door. The guard places their hand on a black panel and the door opens, then bows and walks away. Carter steps inside as the door closes behind him.

He looks around and sees posters of different bands and singers. Toward the back wall, Carter can see a queen bed with dressers on both sides. The floor is wooden compared to the thin carpet that runs everywhere else. There are rugs scattered around the place of varying colors. Carter looks to his right to see a shoe rack on the ground. On top of it lies a caddy filled with miscellaneous things. He notices a quarter, picks it up, and tries to roll it across his knuckles, only getting about halfway before he loses it and tries it again. He stops and sets it down, then walks deeper into the room, taking a seat on the bed. He hears Dawn quietly singing along to music in another room. He knocks on the door, and the singing and music stops.

"Dad, I'm almost ready. Stop rushing me, please."

"It's me. Your dad sent me up here while Lola enjoys the buffet he set up."

"Carter?! I, um— Don't come in. I'm not ready yet!"

"I figured that out. I'll wait for you." He walks back to the bed, but stops as he sees a Katana hanging on a wall. "What do we have here?" The blade's sheathe is wrapped in a dark red leather with a white cloth wrapped around the top half of the sheath and a handle that's double the length of a traditional blade. Carter takes it off the rack and slides the blade halfway out to see a scarlet red blade. At the base of the blade, there are two Japanese characters Carter doesn't recognize. He closes his eyes and rubs the blade. "No karma; this blade hasn't been used."

"What hasn't been used?" Dawn asks. Carter turns around swiftly, still holding the sword. He looks at Dawn, wearing an oversized shirt and shorts with her hair done up nicely, with a bit of makeup on her face.

"Oh, this sword. It's very pretty. There are no signs of use on it," Carter says, putting it back on the rack with the handle on the left side of the rack.

"Well, duh. I don't go LARPing like you do. Plus, I wouldn't dare use Vermillion. Her blade is too pretty to be used," Dawn says, stepping into a large walk-in closet.

"I do not LARP! Just because I participated in a renaissance fair one time, I'm automatically called a LARPer?!"

"Yep, pretty much." Dawn giggles while pulling out a dress. Carter sits down on the bed and stares at the sword.

"So are you and your dad gonna move back to your old house, or is this a permanent thing now?"

"Unfortunately, it seems like it's permanent," Dawn says from the closet. "Ever since that break in, he doesn't want to go back there just in case something like that happens again. This place is under twenty-four-hour surveillance, and the whole floor of this building is all for me and my father." Dawn comes out of the closet in a long black dress that looks like it spirals around her like a tornado, holding a pair of heels in her hand. "Carter, you don't have to keep looking away. I'm dressed now."

"Okay, well how about we—" Carter stares at Dawn. His eyes look up and down, saving every detail in his head. "You look … amazing."

"I, um … well, thank you." Dawn moves her hair in front of her face, hiding her embarrassment. "Can you help me finish getting ready?"

"Sure, what do you need?"

"Can you help me put my heels on and then fasten the back of my dress?" Dawn turns around, revealing her open back. Carter nods and approaches her gently, grabbing the strings and pulling them until they're tight, quickly knotting it. She looks up at a mirror on her wall to see Carter's face turning a faint red, but smiles and lets him finish. After he's done, she sits down on the bed and pulls her dress up a little, holding her feet out. Carter

quickly puts the heels on and stands up.

"Are you all ready to go now?" Carter walks over to the

door.

Dawn smiles and walks over to him. "Yes, I'm ready." She kisses his

cheek, then makes her way down the hall. Carter shakes his head

and catches up to her. The two stop and wait for the elevator.

Dawn's whole face is a deep red, and she refuses to look any other

direction besides forward. The elevator doors open and Dawn

disappears into it. Carter joins her and the two go down in silence.

Darson Shardlow

Chapter Twelve

Carter and Dawn rejoin the party, and soon after, the main lights go out and music begins to play. The two turn their gaze to the stage that was set up. A spotlight turns on Mr. Shardlow as he does a cheesy dance up to a microphone that rests on a stand. The crowd cheers and claps while he makes his way over.

"Thank you all for coming! I know this was rather sudden, so I appreciate every single one of you for still coming to hear the news." Mr. Shardlow takes the microphone out of the stand and paces along the stage. "Now, what news could be so great that a party was necessary? Well, as my main business partners and future partners, I would like to announce Iron Works' next plan of operation." He turns around and a screen lights up. "Starting next month, we will be releasing two lines of products as part of our company's new medical branch. We are calling it the Singular

Tonic Injection Mechanism Pack—or the STIM pack, for short." He gestures to the screen, which now displays a syringe with a short needle and a more mechanical body.

"This device can instantaneously trigger the healing process within the human body to help stop wounds and regenerate cells so the body stays ready for anything. We're planning on introducing three variants of the product for different grades of needs." The screen turns from one of the syringes to three of varying designs. "We'll first launch our public variant. This version of the product has the smallest dose to help in everyday scenarios, such as a cut in the kitchen or an unfortunate accident with tools in the backyard. Then we will launch both the medical and military variants at the same time. These two variants are very similar but have slight variations. The medical one is the strongest of the three, which is used for patients who have suffered large wounds such as being impaled or crushed by heavy objects. Since it's the strongest, it can only be used once a day to be considered safe. Any more in a day can cause overdose side effects, but one of our goals is to improve that time limit.

"The military one is a fast-acting formula. This variant works three times as fast, but because of this, the body does not have enough time to replenish enough blood, so the soldier may be a little loopy, but they will live. We have tested and confirmed that this variant can heal bullet wounds. We are unsure if a head shot can be fixed, and we have refused to test that for the sake of our test subjects, who bravely volunteered for the future of our world's health care."

Mr. Shardlow faces the crowd as they all cheer with excitement. Carter turns and sees Dawn is missing. He turns and his eyes lock on her as she stands on the side of the stage, holding a box. The guards don't seem to be paying attention to him, but rather to Mr. Shardlow. Carter pulls out his list, reads through it, and makes his way back into the elevator. Before he steps on, he looks at his shoes and thinks for a moment. He checks for cameras, but doesn't see any. As he steps in, he transforms into Karma. He looks through the floor numbers and sees it doesn't go lower than that floor. Carter notices a metal panel below the buttons and places his hand on it. The elevator door shuts and the lights at the top of the elevator turn off and strips of lights at the bottom light up.

"Welcome, Carter Shadson," the elevator voice says. He looks around and then the buttons change labels from floor numbers to text for all the different departments of the company.

"I have a bad feeling about this." Carter looks at the button that says *Weapons Development*. He presses it and the elevator moves downward. It stops and the doors open. He steps out into a wide hall with a large glass window on the left, looking out onto a warehouse-sized room filled with men in lab coats and safety equipment. He pulls out his phone and takes pictures of the weapons they are testing. "Those are definitely Rood Staal weapons," Carter says to himself. A man in a lab coat observes as a glass jar with spider-like robotic legs crawls onto a box. The box disappears and then reappears. Three men play a game of darts, and even though one of the men throws unconventionally, his throws aim the most true. "That guy is good."

Carter takes a few more pictures, then returns to the elevator. He goes down another floor and walks into a smaller room filled with metal cabinets full of weapons and armor. He walks through, gazing at the guns and bulletproof vests. He reaches the back and finds a row of cabinets with a red and gold ornamental design, all locked. He summons his sword and swings it at one of the locks, breaking it off. Carter then uses his two swords folded to open the cabinet doors. After a few struggling attempts, he opens the doors and peers in. Inside are multiple Rood Staal short swords and a row of STIM packs.

"Clearly, he provided his soldiers with some prototypes." Carter carefully grabs one, making sure not to touch the others or anything else in the cabinet. He takes a picture and closes everything back up. He notices a door in the corner and uses the butt of his sword to push down on the door handle—it doesn't budge. Carter clicks his tongue and bashes his body against the door, opening it. In the new room, there's a single cage with gear inside. Adjacent to it is a workbench filled with tools and blueprints.

Carter walks over to the cage and sees the Titan's armor within. "Hello there." He reaches for it, then stops for a moment and looks at the roof. "Infrared lasers. Damn. If this wasn't a stealth mission, I would just bust this cage open." He turns away and looks at the workbench, where there are several blueprints with armor designs for Titan. "Big arms, wings, jet boots, blades—wait, no, that looks like a helicopter backpack. Are they planning to make more than one Titan or just give them more abilities?" Carter asks, turning his gaze to the side.

His eyes lock onto a helmet similar to Titan's resting on the side of the bench. "This one looks incomplete." He holds it and closes his eyes. "I can't get a reading out of this." Carter moves to the middle of the floor and holds his hand on the ground. He waits for a moment and takes a deep breath.

"That damn kid!" a voice shouts. Carter jumps up in place to see Titan standing near him. "He has no idea what kind of power he possesses!" They walk toward Carter and pass through. Carter turns around and sees Titan sit in a chair, then reaching up to take off their helmet. It clicks and a small hiss of air is released. A roaring cheer shakes the room, making Titan disappear. Carter looks up.

"Damn it. So close. I should hurry back." He rushes back to the elevator. "One more floor." Inside the final floor, Carter finds all the remaining evidence he needs. Tanks, helicopters, prototype mechanized suits, all with *Iron Organization* branded on them. He wastes no time taking pictures and quickly returning to the party. When he reaches the main floor, the elevator's lights and buttons return to normal. He gets out and none of the guards bat an eye at him. Carter walks through the crowd and sees Mr. Shardlow holding a gun and pointing it at a target behind him. He shoots, but not a sound is heard.

"And that, ladies and gentleman, is the end of my little preview of the next line of development. Now, if anyone would like to invest in any of the products I have shown off today, you know how to contact me." Mr. Shardlow bows and the rest of the lights turn back on. Carter sees Dawn talking with her father along with another man. He starts to approach the three when his senses go off, revealing all the karma within the room. Nearly every person in the room, save for a few here and there, has karma built up. He turns to the three and sees Dawn and her father are clean, but the man they are talking to is not. Carter gets closer to them, his brain rattled by the screams of the karma. It then focuses and pin points on one individual, who's admiring the gun Mr. Shardlow demonstrated earlier. The individual grabs the gun and inspects it. There is a guard standing behind the display, monitoring them. Carter's vision identifies the individual as one of the businessmen behind him in line to get into the party. The man's karma flares up.

"That ain't good." Carter grabs an empty plate off a table next to him. The suspicious man quickly shoots the guard watching over them. People nearby freak out and duck out of the way. Everyone turns to the man, who is now aiming the gun at Mr. Shardlow. Carter flings the plate like a frisbee. It crashes into their arms, moving it out of the way and causing them to misfire at a plant. Carter appears next to Dawn, scooping her up in his arms and running down the hall, passing her off to a guard. The guard covers her, along with two others. Carter turns around to see the man pinned to the ground. The room calms as the guards escort the man out of the room and a cleaning crew comes in to take care of the mess made.

"I am so sorry, everyone. I'm sorry you had to see these events unfold right in front of you. If you wish to leave, you may; I wouldn't blame you. Again, I apologize." Mr. Shardlow bows and apologizes profusely to the crowd. About half the crowd gets up and leaves, the rest murmuring about their investment options.

As the chatter calms down and people return to normalcy, Mr. Shardlow tries to mingle with the remaining business partners and bring about something good from the small disaster. He turns and sees Carter standing by a pillar, watching over everyone. He excuses himself and walks over to him. "I guess I didn't need to hire guards, only you."

"Is Dawn okay?" Carter asks blatantly.

"Dawn is a little shaken by what happened, but she did say thank you for what you did, and I want to thank you as well. I know that man was after me, but if he was successful, he probably would have shot her next to remove the company's heir. Thank you for protecting my daughter, Carter. It means a lot to me." He smiles at Carter, holding out his hand.

Carter grabs it and shakes it. "I was just protecting my friend."

"I know things have been hard for you since your parent's passing. I'm just glad to see you pushing through. I remember when Dawn told me about the woman who broke into your house a month later and attacked you with a knife only to feel pity for you after seeing the death confirmation papers of your parents,"

Mr. Shardlow says while taking a sip out of a cup he is holding.

Carter rubs the scar under his right eye, feeling the memories seep in just a little. "What happened to the guard who was shot?"

"Well, thanks to our STIM technology, they'll be back on their feet in a few hours."

"Can I ask you a question?"

"Sure, I don't see why not." Mr. Shardlow turns his head, a curious gaze in his eyes.

"Besides me being friends with Dawn, why invite me to something like this? This isn't the kind of party I would be interested in at all." Carter's eyes meet his and Mr. Shardlow clears his throat and nods his head slightly.

"Carter, you are a very rare type of person. My father used to tell me there'll be certain individuals you meet in your life that just stick out more than others, and those are the people you want by your side regardless of the reason, because making them your enemy would be one of your biggest regrets. You, Carter, you have this presence about you I can't explain. Dawn often says you're a lodestar. You are a natural born leader—someone you have no problem following. She truly believes you could travel to hell and come back," Mr. Shardlow says with a smile.

"What's the real reason?"

"You're smart, I'll give you that. All right, no more buttering you up." He stands up straight and looks Carter in the eyes. "What do you know about the Evil Alliance?"

"I know someone beat me to it."

"So you've seen them too. How many have you seen?"

"I have only seen Karma and Devil," Carter says, listening intently.

"I know your father researched them a lot and Dawn told me your trip to find it was fruitless. Do you have any idea who could have found it before you? Did your father have any colleagues?"

"As far as I know, he only worked on it with my mother, but that was very minimal. According to my mother, it was a project many knew very little about. Lola only knows that he worked on the subject, and what the general public knows," Carter says.

"I think teaming up with the Evil Alliance would be the next step in something better for the world. I feel they would be more useful as diplomats than violent peace keepers. Basically, what I want to offer you is a job here that would allow you to pick up where your father left off, with the added bonus of having new technology and all the information we have. We wish to locate them and be able to converse with them and request their aid for the sake of humanity." Mr. Shardlow grabs Carter's shoulder with a confident smile.

"I don't know. I don't even know if what I found was even remotely close to the temple's location, so I don't know if I could figure out a single moving person's location."

"Hey, no rush. You would work whatever hours you want, and I can negotiate a large salary for you, so have more spending money. Whatever you want, I will make sure I can accommodate. Look, I want to help you. You have helped me so much by being there for my daughter when I can't. I clearly see that when she's with you, she is safe." He smiles and turns his gaze to a woman walking up to him. "Hello, Lola. Enjoy the buffet?"

"Oh, very much so. I think a little too much, but I'll be fine." She giggles. "Come now, Carter, we must be going. It's getting a little late and I wanna go home and crash for the night," Lola says with a smirk. Carter sighs, placing his hand on his face.

"Actually, Lola, do you mind if I borrow Carter for a little bit longer? I could have someone bring you some antacids for your stomach, if you'd like?"

"That sounds nice. I'll be here when you two are done. Just don't take too long, please."

"Of course, it shouldn't be too much longer. Come, Carter. I wish to show you something." Mr Shardlow walks Carter over to the elevator and presses his hand on the panel.

"Welcome, Mr. Shardlow," the elevator says. It moves upward, and the two stand quietly. They stop at the top floor, but the doors don't open. The back wall of the elevator slides to the side, opening up.

"This way, Mr. Shadson." Mr. Shardlow walks into the opened room. Carter steps off the elevator, confused. He steps into a big open room with a large table in the center. In the back of the room are four large television screens that take up the whole wall, displaying a screensaver. Carter approaches the table and sees a map of Parabi city. Along the map are small wooden carvings of buildings. He looks at one of them closely.

"Are these pieces from a board game?" Carter asks with a smirk.

Mr. Shardlow sighs. "Yes. I was trying to get my team to make miniature replicas of our buildings, but they thought it would be funnier if they just got generic board game pieces instead."

"Well, they were right about them being funny." Carter looks at the map from one end of the table.

"These are the last reported locations of the Evil Alliance—at least, here in Parabi. But they were first seen at the summer camp in Aqua Gate, the same time you were there." Mr. Shardlow stares at Carter from the other side of the table. "I assume that's when you first saw them, right?

"It is."

"Only Karma and Devil were reported being seen there, although one person said they saw a third, but they couldn't say with confidence there were actually three." He slowly walks over to Carter. "Then Luck made an appearance recently. We're still waiting for Curse and Jinx to make an appearance, but they seem to be lying low for now." He stops in front of Carter. "That's where I need your help. I need to find the other two. If we have the entire Evil Alliance cooperating with us, we can save millions of lives. We could prevent so much destruction!"

"Or become the cause of it." Carter clenches his fists, staring at the map.

"What did you say?"

"I said: or become the cause of it. Having a force of nature like them as an ally will only invite conflict. By having them tied to a leash, you'll be causing others to rise and attempt to take them or destroy everything because of the sheer power imbalance," Carter says, walking over to a side table with a spread of weapons—most of them your run-of-the-mill firearms.

"You think controlling them will backfire on us?"

"I don't think it will. I know it will." Carter picks up some unique weapons on the end of the table, lying on top of a red cloth.

"May I ask why you believe that, Mr. Shadson?"

"As long as you seek to control, there will be a rebellion to fight back. You will be fighting an unnecessary battle." He picks up a black, boxy pistol. The forward sight has a grayish red hue to it.

"Well, control is a strong word for it. It's really a form of cooperation." Mr. Shardlow fiddles with his hands. Carter presses a button on the front of the pistol, releasing the large magazine, revealing a solid red core inside but no bullets.

"You intend to subdue them using their weakness of Rood Staal." Carter looks over at Mr. Shardlow.

"I'm not surprised you know of it." He smiles and walks over to Carter. "That pistol is our new prototype firearm. That inflicts a heavy stun. While yes, it would hurt us, it would be worse for them."

"I'm sorry, Mr. Shardlow, but if this is your way of approaching the Evil Alliance, I will not help you." Carter stands tall, full of confidence.

"I understand, Carter. I knew it was a long shot, knowing how you feel about things, but I appreciate you hearing me out. Now, we should be getting back down. Don't want to keep Lola waiting any longer." Mr. Shardlow walks over to the elevator, joined by Carter. They ride down in silence, then step out and meet back up with Lola, who is sitting in a chair. Carter helps Lola to her feet.

"Well, Mr. Shardlow, it was a lovely party." Lola's face brightens as she reminisces about the wonderful food.

"I'm glad you had a good time. You two have a good night. And Carter, if you reconsider, you are always welcome." Mr. Shardlow bows and returns to his guests while Carter hurries Lola out of the party. As Mr. Shardlow talks to his guests, the man he was conversing with before the shooter approaches him.

"Ah, Mr. Fulk. What can I help you with?" Mr. Shardlow asks.

"We have the data you requested ready."

"Oh, excuse me. I will be right back." Mr. Shardlow apologizes to the guests and walks off to the side, away from prying ears. "So what's the word?"

"A singular STIM pack was stolen, but nothing else."

"Did the thief leave any evidence?" Mr. Shardlow folds his arms.

"Yes and no, sir." Fulk clears his throat. "There were no foreign fingerprints detected anywhere within the areas of concern, and as for our shoe print detection system, the shoes that were found were not of anyone here among our staff or guests."

"So you're telling me we have no leads on the identity of the thief?"

"Unfortunately, that is correct."

"Damn, all right. Let's play it by ear. Have another investigation and try to narrow it down as much as possible. Were any profiles used on the elevator?" Mr. Shardlow asks, getting closer to Fulk.

"Oh, yes. There were the regular employees, yours, and one profile that didn't have a name, only a code."

"Was the code linked to anyone?"

"Yes … you. The code was linked to you. It was a profile created through your personal computer."

"All right. Thank you, Fulk. You may go." Mr. Shardlow thinks to himself while Fulk leaves. He stops and returns to his guests.

As Carter opens the door to the car, allowing Lola to get in, he stops and looks back at the building. His eyes reach the top, where a dark figure stands with what looks like a cape billowing in the wind. Carter rubs his eyes and looks back, but the figure is gone. He shrugs and gets into the car for the ride home.

The two arrive at Carter's house. They converse for a moment more before parting ways for the night, with the promise of seeing each other on Monday. Carter unlocks his door and walks in to see Jimena, Logan and Leonidas watching TV on his couch.

"I see my TV was more of a concern than being on standby." Carter locks the door behind him and sets the STIM pack on the table.

"Sorry, Carter. You didn't say much to any of us, so we thought you hadn't found anything yet," Jimena says, turning things off. The three go to the table and look at the STIM pack.

"So what's this?" Logan asks, picking it up.

"That is the new thorn in our side. They call it a STIM pack. Basically, a health regeneration potion from a video game. So now if we strike them down, they have the opportunity to get back up if they don't die."

"Meaning, if you don't intend to end their life, they will take yours," Leonidas says.

"Carter, I don't know how I feel about taking someone's life. I don't mind wounding or disarming them, but to end their life … It's not right," Jimena says.

Carter clenches his fists. "Then you won't have to." He sighs and looks at the three. "I will shoulder that responsibility. If it's deemed necessary, I will end their life." Carter's words widen everyone's eyes. He pulls out his phone and sets it on the table. "Now, as for my little investigation, I have plenty of evidence to connect them both. And as for more concerns, we now know their plan."

"Oh, and what's that?" Leonidas asks.

"They intend to capture and control us with fancy new tech they're building, like more advanced weapons. Anything to stop us in our tracks and then use us to threaten every other country to force world peace. Mr. Shardlow says he wishes to find us for the sake of the world, but with the way he's going about it, I'm pretty sure that was just his attempt to sway me to join his company so they can track us. They've already kept note of where we've appeared, even when we were at summer camp. Luckily for us, he thinks the other two members are out but in hiding, so they might not make a move until they can get us all in one go."

"So from what I am understanding, from what we know, they want to create a super army using the powers of the Evil Alliance?" Logan asks.

"Looks like it." Leonidas turns away and scratches his chin.

"Well, gang, looks like we solved the mystery of their plans." Logan chuckles. "They decided to go the movie trope route and make super soldiers."

"Whether that's their plan or not, whatever it is, we cannot let them succeed. If it comes down to it, I will use Dawn to get what we need."

Chapter Thirteen

Day by day, the group attends school, lying low as much as possible to gather information. They scope out and monitor stores run by Iron Works and follow cargo flow patterns, discovering what they regularly ship to the headquarters to get as many ideas on how to foil their plans and keep themselves alive. The three sit outside the Ironworks headquarters at a nearby cafe with notebooks on the table and their school bags with them.

"So far, all we know is that they get large supplies of raw materials. Mainly base compounds they probably use to craft all their toys." Logan lays his head down on his notebook. Carter taps his pencil against his book, covered in numbers. Jimena pulls out her laptop from her bag and starts typing. The two boys turn and look at her.

"I'm putting the mixed up letters we saw into an unscrambler to see if that tells us what's in them," Jimena says while typing.

"How would that help? Some of them didn't have any vowels," Logan asks.

"Unless they aren't supposed to be words, but elements on the periodic table. A good portion of them don't have vowels, and by having them under a periodic name, most people may look over them like it's nothing. Since they're a big company, them requesting raw materials be sent to their headquarters where the vast majority of their prototyping is done, along with the fact that they're actually running a normal business on the side, gives them the perfect camouflage." Carter stands, excited about his quick discovery.

"Yeah, no. I was joking about the unscrambling. I was just entering the information I have onto a document so I can look into it later while on a private connection, not off a cafe's discount fast food Wi-Fi." Jimena finishes typing, then shuts her laptop. Carter sadly slides back into his chair. "Hey, don't be so glum about it. I will actually look into what you said as well, 'cause you do have a fair point."

"I thought I heard familiar voices." The three turn to where the voice came from and see River standing there, holding her school bag.

"River, is that you?" Jimena stands up quickly.

"In the flesh, girlfriend." River smiles and the two go and hug each other.

"Carter, I know you said you saw her again, but you refused to mention her glow up!"

"I'm sorry; I didn't find the information relevant at the time," Carter says, putting his stuff into his bag.

"Not relevant? Look at her!" Jimena gestures to all of River.

"Stop, you're making me blush. But look at *you*, girl. You look better than me!" River says.

Logan looks the two up and down. "Carter, they both kind of have a point. I mean, why bother to go looking for a girl when there are these two hot pieces right here?" Logan chuckles for a moment. "I'm kidding, of course. You two are lovely, but not my type," Logan says, sliding his stuff away.

"Well, Carter? Are you gonna say anything?" Jimena asks. Carter looks at River for a moment. His gaze causes River to turn her face slightly, refusing to make eye contact while hiding her hands behind her back.

"Her appearance has, in fact, matured into something greater than when we were young children." Carter smirks.

"Safe answer. Good job," Logan whispers to him. Jimena gives the two an angry glare. Logan sees this and holds up his hands, pretending to surrender.

"Hey, where's Dawn? She's normally glued to Carter," River asks.

"She had something she had to do with her father, so we came here to drop her off," Carter says.

"Makes sense. Being the daughter of a businessman must be tough." River smiles. "So, what do you guys have planned for the rest of the day?"

"Well, we were gonna—" Carter's mouth gets covered by Jimena's hand.

"I was talking to the guys about going to the football game happening at mine and Logan's school. We wouldn't go there for the game, but as an excuse for our parents to let us stay out without having to worry. If you'd like to join us, you're welcome to."

"Really? I would love to!" River hugs Jimena again. The two smile and get their stuff ready. Logan and Carter shrug and play along. The four head to the parking lot nearby, stopping in front of Carter's motorcycle and a white four-door car.

"Well, I'll see you guys there." Carter pulls out his foldable helmet and gets ready to put it on.

"Why don't you let River ride with you?" Jimena asks.

"Why would I need to? Logan drives a four-door."

"I don't think she's ridden on your motorcycle before. I think she would enjoy it," Jimena says, nudging River forward.

"I, um … I would like to ride with you, Carter. I've never ridden on a motorcycle before." River's eyes never make contact with Carter's. He scratches at the peach fuzz on his chin, looking away for a moment.

"Uh … all right." Carter walks over to River and puts the foldable helmet on her head. "If I get pulled over for not wearing a helmet, you two have to pay for my ticket."

"Duly noted," Logan says. Carter throws both of their bags in the back of Logan's car. They all get ready to leave. River wraps her arms around Carter, holding onto him tightly.

"Hey, Carter." Logan rolls down the window with a smile.

"What now?"

"Wanna take the tunnels and see who gets there first?"

"Oh, you are on!"

"Wait, what's the tunnels?" River asks in a panic.

"It's a side street with no stops," Jimena says from the other side of the car. Logan smiles, putting the window back up. The two roll out onto the street and make their way to the road before stopping at the only stop sign that lies at the beginning of the tunnels.

"Carter, is this safe?!" River asks. Carter turns his head to face her.

"Not at all." Carter smiles and turns to Logan. The two nod as another car passes by, going the other direction. The two punch it, launching from the start. River holds on tighter, locking her fingers together. The two speed down the road, zipping past buildings. They scurry off, going as fast as possible without going overboard. River looks ahead and sees a large tunnel as the two race into its dark abyss. "Hold on tight, River!" Carter shouts. The two turn on their lights, and River sees the tunnel curves slightly but goes down as well. Her face grows fearful and she grabs on tighter. Carter feels her against his back and his mind goes blank for a second as he almost runs into Logan. He snaps out of it and slides back, spinning around and coming to a complete halt.

The two watch as the car drives away. Carter grunts and goes full throttle. The tires screech as they launch from their spot. River grips tighter as they quickly climb in speed. They catch up to Logan and Jimena in no time.

They exit the tunnel, and the bright light of day explodes in their faces. River keeps her eyes closed for a moment, slowly opening them as she feels them slow down and move back onto normal streets. A few minutes later, the two arrive at the school and park. River gets off the bike, and her legs tremble as she almost falls to the ground. Carter catches her before she hits the ground and gets her to her feet. He takes off the helmet. "You okay?" The two lock eyes for a moment.

"I … Yeah." River tries to say anything else, but nothing leaves her mouth. A car honks, and the two turn and see Logan and Jimena pull up. They get out of the car.

"Nice of you to join us." Carter stands up straight, still supporting River in his arms.

"Yeah, yeah, yeah. Speed demon." Logan shuts his car door. "You only won 'cause I got stuck at a red light because the doofus in front of me didn't read the right turn only sign."

"Sure, that's what it was … not that you were just slow."

Carter chuckles. Jimena goes over to River and helps her stand by

herself.

"You okay, River?" Jimena asks.

"Yeah, it was just … a lot."

"Sorry, I shouldn't have encouraged them."

"No, no, you're fine. I was fine with them doing it, I just

didn't expect to go that fast. I think that was technically the fastest

I have ever moved, 'cause none of the rollercoasters I have ridden

ever got that fast." River holds her head for a moment, then lets

go. The four gather themselves and head into the school, making

their way through the crowded bleachers to find a spot. They sit

where they can and watch the game for about an hour, enjoying

each other's company and properly taking the time to catch up

with each other about the past few years they've missed.

"Carter, River? Could you guys go get us some drinks and snacks?" Jimena asks the two with a smile.

"Okay. You gonna give us money?" Carter asks.

"Sorry, I spent my money at the café."

"You bought a cup of ice water and a cup of whipped cream for someone's dog, which cost you less than five dollars."

"I'll pay you back later, okay? Just go get it."

"Fine. Come on, River," Carter groans as he gets up and the two walk away.

"Why do you keep making them do things together?" Logan asks.

"I'm just trying to help a girl out. She would do the same for me if there was someone I liked." Jimena smiles, watching the game.

"Is there even someone you like? I don't think I've ever seen you interact with anyone romantically since that one guy a few years ago— Hold on, why can't I be your wingman?!"

"Because you're terrible with women. What makes you think I would ask you for dating advice?"

"Hey, I'll let you know I'm *not* bad at dating. That's Carter!"

"Oh yeah? Then how come he has two girls vying for his attention?" Jimena smirks as she looks at Logan.

He opens his mouth then closes it, thinking to himself. "Damn, I hate when you're right." Logan pouts.

"Oh, relax. I'm pretty sure Dawn's just in love because they're childhood friends and she doesn't know how to break down those emotions into how she really feels. And as for River, it's currently a rekindling of an old crush she had on him after meeting him again, so I doubt either of them would be dating anytime soon," Jimena says, looking at her hands. "I don't think they could handle his complex mind. I can barely understand him sometimes."

"What do you mean by that?" Logan tilts his head.

"I don't know fully." Jimena adjusts herself and turns toward him. "Ever since we got our powers, when I touch people, it's like I can read their emotions. Like I can see where they are emotionally and what they feel toward others."

"Is that one of your powers?" Logan scoots closer.

"I would think so. I don't know the full extent of it unless there's something I'm missing, but for right now, it just seems like that's all I can do." She fidgets with her fingers. "So when I touched Dawn earlier when we dropped her off, I could feel a sense of love, but like a confused love. Like she knows she loves Carter, but is not fully sure why she does. And as for River, it's more of a comforting love. Like she enjoys the familiar feeling of his presence, but there's a hint of something new. Like an ember in a small fire." Jimena recounts the moments she experienced. "Before our powers, it was always hard to read Carter. He's become very closed off emotionally since his last break up and parents passing."

"That's true. He always shuts down if someone brings it up. Even when Lola does it," Logan adds.

"Even after getting powers, when I touch him to sense something from him … it's like when a TV gets static. Nothing but a mess. Every once in a while, I'll get a black-and-white picture, given the right circumstances, but that's it. Only an idea, not the full experience. A hollow image lacking color and life." Jimena looks down at her hands, pondering her words.

"So, is Carter's mind broken or something?"

"No, not broken. At least, I don't believe so. It's more like … he runs on a different signal. His mind just operates differently to ours."

"Wow, that was poetic. Can you try it on me?" Logan asks, holding out his hand. Jimena sighs and grabs his hand, then takes a few deep breaths. Logan waits with an awkward expression.

"You like Britney from calculus? *Why?* She's an annoying brat!" Jimena asks.

"I, um … It's like a kind of attraction, I guess," Logan says, stumbling over his words. Jimena scolds him. Meanwhile, Carter and River reach the snack bar.

"So, what do you want, River?" Carter looks at all the items available for purchase.

"I don't know, really. This was kinda sprung on us."

"Tell me about it. Are you hungry at all?"

"A little." River eyes the snacks. Carter looks at her for a moment, then goes up to the counter and orders a few things. A few seconds later, Carter hands her a bag of gummy cola bottles and water.

"You still like those, right? I remember you used to always have those in your lunch box."

"I … I still like them. I'm surprised you remembered because we never talked about it." River's face reddens. "Thank you."

"You're welcome. Now let's go back to the snack wanters." Carter leads the way back and hands the other two their snacks as they continue to watch the game. An hour later, the game ends and the crowds disperse while the four still hang out on the bleachers, talking for a bit more before heading back to the parking lot.

"River, do you want Carter to take you home?" Jimena asks, looking at Carter.

"If you want, River, I can take you home." Carter holds his helmet out to her.

"Normally, I'd say yes, but I don't think I could handle another ride on that thing today," River says with a smile. "Thank you, though. And thank you for the snack." She smiles and gets into Logan's car. Logan hands Carter his stuff and the four part ways for the night.

Leonidas

Chapter Fourteen

Carter rides along, making his way home, when the sound of a gun throws him off and scares a nearby crowd, causing a panic. Carter swerves out of the way and gets to a safe spot to get off his ride. More gun shots go off. He moves closer to the sound and sees a man carrying a pistol running away from an alley. Carter gets ready to chase the man when four people wearing white cloaks chase after him. He looks down the alley where they ran out of and sees two people in the white cloaks on the ground in a pool of blood. Carter walks down the alley, keeping an eye out for anyone watching. He doesn't see anyone, so he activates his armor and rushes over to one of the bodies. He flips them over and sees they're wearing a smooth gray mask with two angular eye holes under the cloak's hood. Carter takes off the mask, revealing a woman with lifeless eyes. He notices a chain around her neck and pulls it a little, dragging out what's attached to it. There in his hand is a silver pentagon with different symbols at each point of the pentagon.

"Is that what I think it is? Two swords, pitchfork, axe, scythe, whip ..." Carter flips the woman over and notices the same symbols on the back of the cloak. He rips off the necklace and stashes it in his pocket, then pursues the five who ran away. He eventually reaches a gated community and sees blood on top of the fence. Carter leaps over and dashes in. He catches up and sees the four cloaked people standing there in front of the man, who is now on the ground against a tree, covered in blood.

"This is the last time you get away. You will no longer kill our members." One of the cloaked individuals steps forward and points a curved sword at the man. The man spits out blood and laughs.

"You cultists are nothing but people who want to watch the world burn. You are no better than your average criminal!" the man says.

"Why, you—" The cult member raises the sword. A gunshot rings out, and the cultist's head explodes as they fall to the ground. The four turn and see Carter standing there, holding his summoned pistol.

"It's Karma! Get him!" The three remaining members rush toward Carter, who wastes no time and shoots the three. He disappears his gun and rushes over to the wounded man.

"Karma, is that really you? Did you shrink?"

"What? No, I don't think I did." Carter checks the man's wounds.

"You sound different, too."

Carter's eyes widen, and he turns to the man. "You knew the previous Karma didn't you?"

"You're a new one?" The man coughs. "I knew him as an ally. He would come to our guild and ask my friend Darius for help. Here, take these." The man hands Carter his gun and a red coin. "Go to Darius. He can help you. Stop the cultists. They will do whatever it takes to destroy everything for their own selfish goals." The man tells Carter the address, then passes on. Carter stands up and holds the two items in his hand. The gun is a regular common pistol, while the coin is made of a red plated metal with a bird engraved into it. Police sirens blare, and their flashing lights appear nearby. Carter dashes away, returning to his motorcycle and riding off. Minutes later, Carter arrives at the address given to him by the dying man—a small knick-knack shop. He activates his armor and knocks on the door.

"Don't you see the sign? We are closed!" a voice shouts from inside. Carter pulls out the coin and presses it against the window on the door, then knocks again. The door opens, and in

the doorway stands a tall African man with long dreadlocks,
wearing a grease-covered apron. His dark eyes reach Carter's
mask. "Karma? Come in come in." The man closes the door and
covers the windows after Carter comes in. Carter looks at the
wall-to-wall shelves of products with a bar on one side and a
workbench behind it. "You look different, Karma."

Carter turns around to face him. "That's because I'm not
the Karma you and your friend knew. I am the new Karma, and
your friend gave me these and this address with his dying words."
Carter pulls out the gun and holds the coin in his other hand. The
man is taken aback for a moment, holding his hand over his heart
and clenching his fist tightly.

"That knucklehead. He was being too risky."

"You must be Darius, then." Carter sets the two items on
the table.

"I am, and I assume you need the guild's or my help with something just as the previous Karma did." Darius looks at Carter.

"Could I ask you some questions?" Carter sits on a stool, soon joined by Darius on another.

"Before anything, prove to me you really are Karma and not just some kid working for those cultists," Darius says.

"Fair enough." Carter stands up, walks away, turns his back toward Darius and deactivates his armor for a moment, then makes it reappear. He then sits back down on the stool. "Will that suffice?"

"Yes, it will. Ask away."

"Who were those people in the white cloaks? Who was the previous Karma, and what help could you offer me?"

"For starters, I swore to the previous Karma I would never reveal anything about him to anyone, regardless of the situation. Next, those cultists are a part of … well, a cult called Heinous

Hearts. They are followers of the Evil Alliance, but not in a good way. They want the Evil Alliance to rule the world, but they kill and torture people just for information. They're clever enough to manipulate the government powers to get what they want. The thing is, they are like weeds. You try to kill them, but they just keep sprouting up. The previous Karma instructed me and my friend to provide the firepower and rally an army to stop them. Sadly, the plan only half worked and there are very few of us now. He did say he had some kind of defense against them, but he never mentioned it fully to me."

Darius walks over to a wall with three shelves. He pulls out a piece of metal and it unfolds, doubling its length. He slides it between one of the gaps between the shelves, and the middle shelf lowers into the floor, revealing a passageway. "Come with me." Darius enters the passageway and Carter follows. They reach a door at the end, then enter and turn on the lights. Carter's eyes look upon a weapons arsenal fit for an army. Firearms of all varieties cover the walls, with melee weapons scattered throughout. "This is what I can offer to help you and your comrades." Darius smiles.

"Wow." Carter looks through everything, amazed at the variety and number of weapons.

"Is there something you want? I don't mind giving something to you. It's the least I can do for you bringing back my friend's stuff and the news of his death. Plus, I think the previous Karma would be mad at me for not helping you out." Darius follows Carter as he stops in front of some pistols.

"What's up with this one? It looks like a standard 1911, but different," Carter says, inspecting it.

"Ah, that one. You're right, it's a modified 1911. I call it Kismet. It was actually a custom request from Karma, but he never got to use it. I think it would suit you. One moment." Darius goes over to a cabinet and comes back with a brown leather holster.

"Take this too. You'll probably get more use out of these than anyone else." Darius puts the gun and two extra magazines in the holster. The two leave the room, and Carter shakes Darius' hand.

"Thank you, Darius. And again, I'm sorry about your friend."

"No problem. Just promise that when you take them down, burn the roots down to the core so nothing remains," he says, his voice strained with hatred.

"Don't worry. There will be nothing left when I'm done with them," Carter says, getting on his motorcycle.

"Hey, Karma!" Darius shouts as he tosses something through the air.

Carter turns and catches it. He looks down to see a bundle of remote explosives. "What are these for?"

"You never know when you'll need to blow something up."

Darius smiles, then goes inside. Carter throws them into his bag

and rides off. After he arrives home, he puts his stuff away and

pulls out his notes from earlier. He goes over them, then Leonidas

appears and sits at the table with Carter.

"You had a busy day." Leonidas smirks.

"Do you have something important to say or are you just

going to pester me?" Carter looks at Leonidas with an annoyed

glare.

"I was gonna ask if you need any help with your stuff."

"Actually, you can help me. I need you to find as much

information on the previous Karma and his possible whereabouts.

I met with an old acquaintance of his, but he's keeping it a secret,

which I respect, so I'm not going to force it out of him, especially

after he gave me a nice gun." Carter looks at Leonidas.

"All right, I can do that. It may take me a few days, but I'll do my best."

"Take your time. I can wait." Carter thanks Leonidas, and he disappears. Carter pats his lap for a moment, then stands up. He goes into his backyard and activates his armor. His gaze lowers to the ground to see a handmade training dummy that has been beaten to the ground after several days of use. He turns his sight to the corner of the yard and stares at a tree, then pulls out one of his swords and holds it over his shoulder. He throws it, the sword spinning through the air and sinking into the tree's trunk. He raises his hand. "Come back to me, sword," Carter says to himself.

The sword remains in the tree. "Come! Come to me! Come to my hand!" Carter shouts again, but the sword doesn't move. "Return!" he shouts, and the sword disappears. His eyes widen and he trots over to the tree, only to see the indent of where the sword was. Carter rubs his fingers over the gash. He looks over his shoulder and sees his sword back in its sheath, but also *not* at the same time. He reaches for it, but his hand phases through it. After a moment, the sword solidifies and Carter can touch it. He pulls the same sword out and launches it into the distance. The blade spins through the air like a helicopter as it travels into the sky. Carter reaches his hand out. "Return!" The sword vanishes again.

A few moments pass, and the sword appears in its sheath again. Carter repeats the process a few times, experimenting with it.

"So just thinking of its return will do it. Wonderful. Now, as for the gun." Carter summons his pistol. He stares and admires the detail of the gun the power of Karma has created. He holds it up and aims at the same tree, then pulls the trigger. Its light hum is loud, but not deafening enough to raise suspicion. Carter unloads the gun into the tree until it begins to click.

He walks over to the tree and sees the spread of holes with no bullets present. He fiddles with the gun, realizing there's no release for the magazine. He makes it disappear and then reappear. Then he aims at the tree and fires a single bullet, but the gun again clicks every time he tries to pull the trigger. He puts the gun away and waits a few minutes, fiddling with his phone to pass the time. He pulls the gun out again and is able to shoot a few more shots, but not a full round. Carter nods, looking at the gun before making all of his equipment disappear before heading inside.

Chapter Fifteen

Carter opens his eyes to his dark room—it's only two in the morning. He rolls back over and closes his eyes once more, but is awoken by a clicking sound. He slides out of his bed and undoes a lock on his door. Before he leaves the room, he looks at the lock in confusion. He sets it down and slowly opens the door, looking down the dark hallway. Carter creeps down through the hall, clenching his fists. He reaches the living room and spins around, looking everywhere.

"Leonidas, is that you?" Carter asks the darkness around him. The back door creeps open slowly. He spins toward the sound and watches as a figure cast in shadows slowly pushes open the door, allowing them to slither inside. The figure moves from the door, inching toward Carter. A car's lights flash into the house as it drives by, revealing a woman holding a knife in her hand.

Carter's eyes widen as he tries to summon his armor. Nothing

appears, and the woman swings the knife through the air, slicing

Carter under his right cheek. His face bleeds like a curtain flowing

down a stage along his face. He stumbles and falls onto the

ground, backing up against a wall. His hands shake as he tries to

summon any of his weapons. The woman gets closer, then stops

to look at the table for a moment.

"Oh no, your parents died?" The woman gets closer to

Carter, spreading her legs over him as she sits down on top of him.

She presses the knife to his other cheek. "I can be your new

mommy if you want." The woman chuckles while moving the knife

into the air. Carter looks down at the woman's side and sees

something dangling from it. He tries to focus on it and notices it's

the same necklace one of the Heinous Hearts cultists had. His eyes

widen more as the woman swings the knife down into his chest.

"Gah!" Carter jumps out of bed and stumbles onto the floor. The sun is shining into his room. Carter holds his chest, feeling his heart pound furiously while looking around the room with a hazy gaze. The door handle to his room rattles. Carter backs up, slowly scooting across the floor to the corner of his room. The door opens, and a figure rushes over to Carter.

"Carter, it's okay! It's okay, it's okay. I'm not going to hurt you. Everything is okay. You are safe!" a feminine voice says.

"No, get away!" Carter screams. The figure's hands reach out to Carter. He grabs their wrists and tightens his grip. They continue closer to Carter until they embrace him in a tight hug.

"You're okay, Carter. I'm your friend. I'm not going to hurt you. I promise I won't hurt you!" the voice says calmly, holding Carter. He loosens his grip and lets go, and the arms reach around Carter and begin rubbing his back and the back of his head. His vision returns to normal as he identifies the person. His hands keep shaking, but wrap around them anyway. "It's okay, Carter.

Take your time."

"Thank you." Carter turns his head and locks eyes with

Dawn.

"Same dream?" she asks, still rubbing Carter's back.

"Yeah. It felt worse this time. I felt trapped. Even when I

woke up, I could barely make anything out."

"Carter, I think it's gotten worse. You need help." Dawn

helps him to his bed. "You look terrible." She rubs his face and

places the back of her hand on his forehead. "You don't seem to

have a fever. Stay home today, Carter. Get some rest. I'll tell Ms.

Morris when I get to school about your absence, along with

helping you find a specialist who will help you this time. I've never

seen it this bad before, either." Dawn begins to leave the room.

Carter looks at her wrists and quickly snatches her hands, pulling

222

her back. "What's wrong, Carter?" She looks confused as Carter rubs his thumbs over her red and quickly bruising wrists.

"Are you okay? I didn't mean to hurt you."

"I'll be okay. I'll have my father send me some STIM to patch me up real quick. You know how he is. If I have a paper cut, he'll do anything to make sure it's gone." Dawn removes her wrists from Carter's hands. "Get back into bed. I'll be right back." Dawn leaves the room and Carter scoots back into his bed, sinking into it for a moment. She comes with a small bowl of fruit and a glass of water she sets on his nightstand. "I have to go now. Eat that when you can, and rest in bed. I'll be back after school with Ms. Morris to check up on you. Rest up," Dawn leaves the room, shutting the door behind her.

A few minutes later, Leonidas appears. "What was that all about?"

"I tend to have nightmares about the day that woman broke into my house and attacked me. Things would have gotten worse if the police didn't arrive because one of the neighbors saw her climbing fences into people's backyards. She's the one who gave me the scar under my eye and the one on my chest." Carter moves his hand away from his chest, revealing a cut above where his heart is. "That dream just makes things worse for me; it torments me. It's part of the reason I'm always up late. I fear sleeping, afraid of that terrifying dream. But this was the first time I've had it since I got my powers. And for some reason, it was worse. Way more lifelike, way more detailed. And the aftereffects were cranked up tenfold."

"It may be a side effect of your powers. Your powers are derived from fragments of evil. Something that can induce darker feelings would make something like a nightmare more powerful."

"This time was crazy. I felt like I was really there again. Everything felt so real, just so horrifyingly real. Wait, you said my powers amplified the dream, right?"

"Yeah. Your powers made you remember every single detail to make it as realistic as possible," Leonidas says. "The powers of the Evil Alliance are amplified by negative feelings. So strong emotions of fear, anger, hatred, even sadness can boost your power, but of course, using such power has negative side effects. That's why you must keep your cool when in a fight or else something unwanted will occur." Leonidas' statement looms heavily over Carter's head as his mind processes things. He then jumps out of bed and gets dressed. "Hey, shouldn't you be resting?"

"And shouldn't you be finding me a lead to the previous Karma?"

Leonidas sighs and bobs his head a little. "Fair point. Whatever you do, don't do anything reckless." Leonidas vanishes. Carter finishes getting ready and eats some of the fruit, putting the rest in the fridge. He gathers his things and hops on his motorcycle, riding off. Around twenty minutes later, he pulls up to a prison. He swallows deeply, then makes his way inside. After a few minutes of waiting, he gets to a visitor check in.

"Hello and welcome to Ferrick's Women's Prison. Who is it you'll be seeing today?" the old woman behind the desk asks, seeming annoyed.

"I'm here to see Aubrey Davids," Carter says, feeling nervous.

The woman types away at her computer and then looks back up to Carter. "And what is your relationship with her?"

"I'm, um … Well, I—"

"Sir, what is your relationship with Miss Davids?"

"I'm her … victim." Carter clenches his fists as the words leave his mouth.

The old lady's eyes widen, and she clears her throat. "Oh, um …

Do we want a meeting between glass or in person today?" Her

voice changes from annoyance to concern.

"In person please," Carter says. She nods and sets

everything up, tapping away on her computer's keyboard. A few

minutes later, he's led to a room by a guard. Carter stops at the

one-way window and sees Aubrey. She's pale and thin, with long

messy brown hair and piercing yellow eyes. The guard opens the

door and Carter walks in. Aubrey's eyes widen as she sees Carter

sit down across from her. "Hello, Aubrey."

"Hello again, Carter. It's been a long time. You certainly

have grown. I never thought you would ever visit me. Is it to make

fun of me or to say you forgive me after all these years?" Aubrey's

blank tone and emotionless expression leave a sour taste in the

air. Carter clenches his fists. His mind races as he knows with his

current power, he could easily decimate her.

"No, it's not. I'm here on business, you could say. I'm here to ask you about this." He holds out his hand, the cultist's necklace dangling from his fist. Aubrey's blank stare turns to fear in a matter of seconds.

"Where did you get that?!"

"I got it from one of your friends. They had no need of it anymore. So now I want to know, why were you at my house that night? The real reason." Carter glares at Aubrey. His eyes shoot hate-filled daggers toward her.

She takes a deep breath and sits up straight in her chair. "Clearly, the cat is out of the bag. Do you mind if I give you some back story real quick?"

"Go ahead."

"I was part of the cult because of my parents. They were followers and wanted me to be a part of it too, so I grew up in it. But after years of it and realizing how restricting it was, I started looking for a way out. Then, that night occurred. I was tasked to reclaim your father's research from the house, but we thought the house was empty. Again, at that point, I was already on the fence about leaving the cult. And when I got there and went inside your home, things happened. When I was given the task, I was told that there could be no evidence and no witnesses. So when you came out of your room, the cult's brainwashing took over a little and I went on attack. But then I saw your face after that swing. Something snapped in me. For some reason, I felt the urge to protect you. That I should make up for what I have done and watch over you in your parents' place. When the police arrived, I panicked, cutting your chest in the process before I was taken away. Unable to explain myself—like that would even make a difference at that point—I didn't resist and allowed myself to be taken in." She lowers her head in shame.

"What was it you were looking for in my father's research?"

"I'm sure you're aware of the previous Karma's final acts."

"Of course. He killed the other four members and disappeared." Carter leans forward. "What does that have to do with my father's research?"

"The Heinous Hearts were the real reason the previous Karma killed the others. Our technology made with a material called Rood Staal was superior to the point that we were able to control the other four members, except for Karma. After the cult's defeat, they were determined to find out why he was immune to the effects of Rood Staal. A few years later, the cult got wind of your father's research and wanted it for themselves, hoping it would lead them to success, or at least to some answers. So they sent me to go retrieve it. None of us knew your parents had passed only a few days prior."

"Thank you. What you've told me helps answer a lot of questions." He stands up and prepares to leave.

"Wait, that's it? That's all?"

"What else were you expecting?"

"I expected you to shout in my face and get mad at me for what I did!"

"In truth, I would love to break your skull in for the trauma you have caused me. The nightmares you have given me of you attacking me and then continuing to taunt and play with me like it was some kind of game for you!" Carter says. He takes a deep breath and composes himself. "But thanks to your nightmares, I was able to piece something together. If it wasn't for that damn nightmare, I would never have known that the person who attacked me all those years ago would be linked to everything I'm currently facing. Although, I didn't expect to learn anything from you today about those cultists. I honestly expected you to just be some crazy lady who likes to mess around and has a weird fashion sense."

"I don't blame you for remembering it differently."

"What do you mean?"

"I never toyed with you. In fact, I started crying after the initial strike." Audrey starts to tear up. Carter sits back down in his chair. "When I was in high school, I fell in love with a kind man. He was great, and I wanted to spend the rest of my life in his warm arms. One day, I found out I was pregnant. I wasn't too worried as it was our senior year and we had only two months left of school. I was excited to be a mother. And then we got into a car accident. Him and the baby didn't make it. I was overwhelmed by my grief. I lost two things I loved so dearly. I wanted to be a mother so badly. I could never find a man I loved as much as I did him. So, time went on and I spent my days alone. Eventually, the day arrived when I was tasked with breaking into your house. I hopped the fences and went to your back door and got inside. Then I saw all of those documents. The article, death reports, everything. It clicked in my head that they thought the house was empty because they saw your parents leave on a trip, not that they had died.

"I heard a noise, and there you were … a young, scared boy standing alone in the dark. That's when the brainwashing kicked in. My mind went blank, and I rushed toward you with my knife. You fell to the ground and backed against the wall. That's when my mind fought back. The brainwashing had broken after years of not going to any of the big meetings, and for a moment, I felt at peace. Then, just like that, I realized what I had done and began to panic. I saw your terrified face, and I started to cry because I had turned into a monster. I became something a mother would never want their child to see.

"I felt terrible and rushed to your side, trying to get you to calm down. You were freaked out, and I'll be honest, there was a part of me that wanted to scoop you up and take you away. I set my knife down and wiped the blood off your cheek, trying to clean you up and make you feel better the best way I knew how. Then the door burst open and the police rushed in. I grabbed my knife and was about to grab you and make a run for it, but they got to me, and during that moment, my knife went into your chest. I was taken away and sent to the slammer.

"I confessed to everything. I told them about the cult, but it turned out that the one interrogating me was a spy for the cult. They sent me here and said the only way I could get out of my 30-year sentence early is if my bail is paid. The only people I thought would help me were my parents, since it was their fault I was a part of that damn cult to begin with. They came, said the cult ordered that I stay put and for no one to pay my bail. So now

I'm here. But hey, I only got about two decades left." She gives

Carter a fake smile.

Carter processes everything he heard. He stops for a

moment and turns his head to the one-way window, then quickly

spins back to Aubrey.

"All right, Aubrey, you're going to tell me where their

hideout is and any of their usual meeting spots."

"What, why? You can't go after them, Carter, they'll kill

you!"

He punches the metal table, making a large dent in it. "I'm not

afraid of them. Now tell me, Aubrey."

She remains speechless for a moment, then adjusts

herself. "Their hideout has probably moved, but it used to be in

the sewer near the power plant. As for their usual meeting spots

for quick meetings or business deals, they do it in parks most of

the time. They have a lot of followers and will often have them fill the parks posing as families to deter others from coming as they will see it's full and will want to go elsewhere. Their favorite park is on the north side of town called Tarlima Park. It's a park that's primarily run down, so it's rarely used by the public. They keep their meetings to Thursdays to keep it consistent." She leans back into her chair.

Carter nods. "Thanks for that. I'll be going."

Aubrey reaches out and grabs his hand. "Carter, what have you become? I never would have thought something I did years ago would turn you into the man I see before me."

"I have begun walking a darker path, one I'm not proud of. I guess you could say it's a path of vengeance, but it's the path I now walk, and one I can't walk away from." Carter clenches his hand around hers.

Aubrey looks into his eyes. A flame of fury burns in his gaze. Then, it all becomes clear to her. "You … You're him. You're the new Karma, aren't you?"

A smirk grows across his face. Aubrey looks at his hand as it becomes encased by a dark red flame. It quickly travels up his body until it completely encases him until his armor is shown. The two stay silent for a moment until he transforms back.

"It makes sense that you would become this. I won't say anything. I owe you that. Please be careful, Carter. You may be strong, but they have numbers. Don't go is my best advice."

"I will see you again soon, Aubrey. That's a promise." He removes his hand and leaves the room.

The guard returns to the door. "Are you all good for the day?"

"I am, thank you." Carter smiles and goes back to the front to sign out, then leaves. He pulls out his phone to see texts from friends and Lola checking in on him. He goes to the group chat he

has with Logan and Jimena and types in a few words: **I got us

something. Get ready.**

River Garnet

Chapter Sixteen

Street lamps light up an empty suburban road as the night sky fills

the rest. Jimena stands atop a rocky hill, binoculars in hand,

looking out down the road. She lowers them, letting them dangle

from a strap around her neck. Slowly, she turns around and makes

her way down the rock mound to Logan and Carter.

"Anything?" Logan asks.

"Nope. Nothing but empty roads as far as I can see."

Jimena leans back and stretches. "Carter, are you sure you can

trust her? I mean, she did try to steal your dad's work, and she

almost killed you." Carter doesn't react or move, he just stares at

his phone. "Carter?"

"Hello, Earth to Carter?" Logan waves his hand in front of

Carter's face, but he just keeps staring. Logan quickly wets his finger and reaches for Carter's ear, but Carter stops him before he can.

"Don't even think about it." Carter gives Logan a death stare.

"Geez, man. Relax. We were just trying to get your attention. What are you so focused on?" Logan looks at Carter's phone to just see a text message chain. "Who are you texting?"

"It's Dawn. Well, I was texting her, but something isn't right." Carter scrolls through some of the messages. Jimena sits up fully and scoots closer.

"What do you mean?" Jimena holds her chin as she looks at the phone.

"Dawn doesn't usually hang out with us on Thursdays as she attends business meetings with her father so she can one day do the meetings on her own to help the business," Carter says.

"Yeah, and?"

"They need to be getting the Rood Staal from somewhere, and with the Heinous Hearts being the main producer, it means Iron Work's is getting their supply from them. Hence the reason we're here to confirm that."

"I don't follow." Logan looks at Jimena, confused.

"What does this have to do with Dawn other than the possibility that she's aware of the dark deals her father is mixed up in?"

"She asked me if I wanted to come with them to their meeting. I declined, obviously, but I wonder what it would have been like." Carter rests his head on his hand. All three of them turn their head and quickly rush to the top of their spot and look out. In the distance, three sets of headlights following one another make their way down the street. As they get closer, their shape becomes clearer—heavily armored vans. The three vans drive past the group and into a parking lot, passing a sign for

Tarlima Park. The vans park with the back doors facing the sidewalk. All three sets of van doors open at the same time, with five Iron Organization grunts coming out of each one, carrying rifles and scanning the park. Titan steps out of the middle van, tightening their belt and walking into the park. The grunts follow, still spread out.

"Do you see what they're doing?" Logan moves his head from side to side, trying to get a look. He turns back to Carter, only to find him missing. "Um, Jimena? Where's Carter?" Jimena passes Logan the binoculars and positions him. Carter stands behind a large tree, clad in his armor. "What is he doing? Is he trying to get spotted?"

"No. He's listening," Jimena says.

Carter slowly creeps his head around the tree to see Titan on the other side of the park.

Titan approaches a public bathroom building and knocks on the *staff only* door, backing away right after. The door opens and three of the white-cloaked members of the Heinous Hearts step out. One holds the door open while the other two stand to either side of the door, holding the same rifles as the Iron Organization. Titan walks through the door, and then all but three of the Iron grunts follow in. Once the grunts are in, the three cult members go back inside.

"What kind of clown car crap is this?" Carter whispers to himself. The three remaining grunts patrol the area. Carter looks back up at the other two and waves his hand.

"That's our cue." Jimena jumps off the hill, transforming mid-air, landing on the ground into a roll and diving behind a tree next to Carter. He nods, giving her a thumbs up. Logan walks down the hill, transforming along the way, then hides behind another tree.

"So what's the plan?" Logan looks out at the three grunts.

"We need to get to that building. Obviously, something fishy is going on. But we can't draw attention, so we need to make sure we get in quietly. Are you guys okay with killing?" Carter asks, but the other two don't respond, eyes darting in different directions. He sighs and holds out his hand to Jimena. "Gimme your pitchfork."

"Um, okay." Jimena reaches to her back, grabs the small pitchfork, and tosses it to Carter. He catches it and makes it expand. He turns to Logan.

"Logan, I'm going to need you to throw your axe over at the lamp."

Logan pulls out his axe, eyes it up, and prepares to throw it. Carter gets ready to sprint, holding up his hand, counting down from five. His hand reaches zero and Logan throws the axe. It flies through the air and smashes right into the lamp's light. The park is instantly engulfed in darkness. The three grunts turn to the lamp with concern, and Carter launches out, the pitchfork flying through the air. It hits one of the grunts, piercing through their chest. As their body hits the ground, the remaining two turn and slowly make their way over. The second they both arrive at the scene, they too fall to the ground. Carter stands behind their bodies, blood dripping from his swords. He shakes as much blood off his swords as he can, then puts them away. He grabs the pitchfork and rips it out of the grunt's body.

"They're dead. You can come out now," Carter says. The two go over to Carter to retrieve their items. "See? Easy-peasy." He walks over to the bathroom, pressing his ear to the door. "There's nothing. There must be a tunnel or something in there." He backs up and tries to rip the door open. "Won't budge." Carter thinks for a moment, then quickly pulls out his swords and rams them between the cracks in the door nearest to the handle.

"Logan, if you would be so kind as to give them a good whack."

"Sure." Logan pulls out his axe, turns it to the flat side, and swings it, smacking the handles of the two swords. The two swords wedge further into the door. Carter backs up a little, then takes a running start and bashes himself into the two handles. The door springs open.

"That shouldn't have worked at all," Jimena says.

"You're right, but who cares?" Carter picks up his swords and notices the plethora of heavy-duty reinforcements on the door, then enters the room. There are normal cleaning materials, maintenance parts, and tools scattered around. In the corner, they spot a staircase going down. The three begin their descent, and upon reaching the bottom, they're greeted by a door. Carter slowly grabs the handle and turns it, but nothing happens.

"Hey, what's that?" Logan touches a symbol indented into the wall. The other two stare at it for a moment.

Carter's eyes widen as he reaches into his coat. He pulls out the cultist's necklace and places it into the groove. They hear a click, and he tries the handle again. This time, the door opens and they see long, wide concrete tunnels.

Carter draws his swords and walks in one of the directions. The other two do the same. The three walk through the tunnel slowly until they reach an opening. The new room they go into has computers lined up next to a window, and on the other side is a workbench with tools and multiple crates filled with miscellaneous parts. Logan goes over to the window as Jimena messes with one of the computers. Carter walks over to the workbench and sees a sword split down the middle with a long metal rod running along the gap. He looks at the base of the sword and spots a metal box with a glass window connected to the rod. Inside the box is a red rock. Carter picks the sword up by the handle and looks at it.

"Why is this in here instead of an armory, or at least a lab?" Carter holds the handle and looks at it again. At the top of the handle, just under the hand guard, is a hook. Carter pulls the hook and a red light covers the metal blade. The light travels from the tip of the blade down to the guard and burns his hand. He quickly pulls the hook again, causing the blade to return to normal. He grabs the box with the rock inside and rips it off the sword, stashing it away in his coat, then returns to the window.

"There's Titan. They're with someone," Logan says, pointing at Titan standing next to someone in a white cloak. The three open a door next to the window that leads to a catwalk in the large tunnel system where Titan is. Along the catwalk are metal panels blocking the railing. The three sneak between them until they get closer to their target to listen in.

"They have the best pretzels at that mall, hands down. Anywho, they're here with your shipment, as requested," a voice says. The cloaked figure next to Titan gestures to two grunts, pulling large stacks of crates with pallet jacks. Titan walks over to the crates and pulls one down. The cloaked person turns around, revealing an extravagant metal mask with horns on their face, distinguishing them from the other grunts. Titan rips open one of the crates—red ore.

"You always know how to get the good stuff, Lothar," Titan says while looking at the red rocks. "That's normally what I would say in this situation, but this is not what we requested."

"I don't know what you are referring to," Lothar says.

"I'm not foolish enough to confuse granite painted red for real Rood Staal!" Titan shouts. Just then, a swarm of Heinous Heart cultists rush to the scene, massively outnumbering the number of Iron Organization members. They all carry the Rood Staal rifle in hand.

"Unfortunately, our supply of Rood Staal comes from our higher ups at headquarters, and they have decided you've lost your usefulness to us, Titan. The Iron Organization is no longer needed to forge our manifesto of the Evil Alliance's rule. We will capture them on our own, thanks to the lovely technology you have graciously given us. I recommend you leave now and tell your boss to hide before we change our mind about keeping you around for our convenience." Lothar cackles as he finishes. Titan starts to walk away, but a second later, they turn, drawing their sword and swinging it at Lothar. Immediately after, lasers begin to fly across the room with both sides taking cover.

"This got out of hand real fast," Logan says and turns to the door they just came from. "Watch out!" Logan shouts, and Jimena turns to see a cult member standing there with a rifle in hand.

They ready their gun, only to be shot in the head. Jimena turns and sees Carter holding Kismet in his hand. Unfortunately, the gunshot gets everyone's attention, who notices the three hiding behind the metal panels.

"The Evil Alliance is here!" someone shouts from the crowd, immediately drawing Titan and Lothar's attention.

"Dammit, they're no fun." Carter chuckles and then ducks, dodging a laser shot as the war below continues. The three take cover once again, with Carter summoning the Pistol of Karma and taking potshots at the swarm below. "This is getting us nowhere." He stands up and picks off one after another, but he takes a laser to his right shoulder and crouches back down.

"If we don't do something, they'll kill us!" Logan shouts. Jimena looks at her two friends, then to the angry crowd of soldiers below. She takes a deep breath and leans to the side of her panel as a red light forms in her hands. A red and gold rifle spawns into her hands. She looks down at the sight of the gun, lining it up with someone below, and pulls the trigger. The gun flashes yellow from the three-prong muzzle, accompanied by the sound of a nail being struck by a hammer, followed by a short whistle as the bullet soars through the air to its target. She continues sending one shot at a time into the crowd. A door behind Logan bursts open and another cultist steps out. Jimena grabs the scope on her rifle and flicks it to the side as an iron sight appears in its place. She holds down the trigger as her rifle unloads into the cultist until they fall to the ground.

"Nice going, girl!" Logan says.

She smiles under her mask, then looks at the rifle in her hands. "How do I get more ammo?"

"You wait. Our weapons work on a regeneration system. The magazine will fill itself again in time, but for now, put it away," Carter says, finishing off the bullets in his pistol and then making it disappear. Jimena turns to the dead cultist in the door behind her and takes the rifle from them, then stands up and holds down the trigger, firing lasers around the room as she moves to the other door.

"You two go that way and try to find anything that can send this place crashing. I've got a play date to supervise," Carter says, hopping over the railing into the battlefield. Logan grabs the rifle off the other cultist, and the two begin their hunt.

Carter runs through the laser firing squads, avoiding as much as he can. He makes it to the other side, where he sees Titan fighting Lothar. Titan uses their Rood Staal Katana, where Lothar just uses a standard issue Heinous Heart sword. Carter draws both of his swords and waits for an opportunity to jump in. The two knock each other back and go back in to strike, only to be stopped by Carter, blocking both of their blades.

"Karma!" Lothar grins under his mask.

"Are you a fan or something?" Carter jokes, then pushes the two away. Both of them stumble before standing up straight.

"Karma, join me now and help me destroy Titan. We can bring about world peace so no one else will have to fight!" Lothar says, clenching his fist.

Carter chuckles for a moment. "As nice as you try to make it sound, I'll have to pass." Carter points one of his blades at him. "A fight now and then makes things more interesting."

"You insolent brat! How dare you interrupt our transaction!" Titan says, stomping one of their feet.

"Are you sure I ended it? 'Cause it looked like this relationship wasn't going to work out anymore." Carter lowers his swords and paces around, almost taunting the two. "I've had a run in with Titan in the past, but you … you're new to me. I'm not the biggest fan of one-way introductions. You already know who I am, so why don't you be a kind lad and tell me who you are?"

Lothar scoffs, then flicks his white coat. "I am Lothar! Leader of the Karma branch of the Heinous Hearts. You will submit to me!"

"Sorry, I ain't a bottom." Carter spins his swords around, taunting the two. "So now that we are all acquainted"—Carter gets into a fighting stance—"let's dance." Lothar chuckles, then drops the sword in his hand and pulls out two swords. The blades are split down the center, creating two prongs.

"You two are insufferable!" Titan shouts, charging toward Lothar. The battle begins, and the two swing their blades against each other. Carter watches for a moment, then rushes behind Lothar and swings. Lothar blocks the swing and spins back and forth between the two, blocking strikes from both Carter and Titan. Carter jumps back for a moment at a standoff, waiting to see who will strike first.

Jimena and Logan dash through halls, scanning the rooms they pass for anything useful, shooting anyone they run into. The two reach one room, and upon entering, a grunt falls from the ceiling on top of Jimena, pinning her to the ground. They raise a red-bladed knife, then swing it down, only for it to explode out of their hand with a boom. They scream in pain as blood pours out of the wound. They turn and see Logan holding a shotgun decorated in the blue and green colors of his armor. Logan pumps the choke of the shotgun and fires again, blasting the grunt off Jimena. Logan helps her up, and the two continue their investigation. The room is filled with computers, and they search them for anything that may help.

"Carter just needs us to destroy this place, right?" Logan asks.

"Yeah. If we destroy the Iron Organization's supply of Rood Staal, we can stop them from creating more weapons, but how to do that is the difficult part." Jimena pulls up a map of the facility on the computer. "This place is huge, so we would need something that will destroy everything without trapping us in the process."

Logan turns around as another grunt walks in, and he shoots them immediately. "I have a feeling that's not the last of them. Keep searching. I'm gonna watch the door." Logan rushes to the door and sticks his head out, looking left and right, shooting any cultist who comes for them.

"I've got it. I have a plan." Jimena slides over to another computer with six monitors, all showing camera surveillance. She flicks through the different cameras until she finds the one pointing toward Carter.

"So, what's the plan?"

"Trying to burn everything won't work because of the lack of combustible objects in here, but there's water moving all throughout the facility. We're going to go to the main water control and make it go haywire, which should destroy and flood the place. Luckily, the process won't be instantaneous, so we'll have enough time to escape through an exit hatch nearby. The only issue is getting Carter out. We went up a few floors trying to get to this room. He's still on the bottom floor fighting." She swings back over to the map and then back to the camera screen. She pulls out her phone. "Carter, can you hear me?"

"Hear you loud and—ugh—clear," Carter says, grunting.

"Look, here's the plan: we have to flood the place. Behind you is a set of stairs that will lead you to a tunnel system. If you keep following the tunnel, it should take you to an exit. You have five minutes until you need to get going, starting now." Jimena turns to Logan. "Let's go."

They make their way to the water control room and stare at two large metal containers with valves at the bottom of them, surrounded by computers. Jimena taps away on the computer. "No use. We'll need to turn the valves manually in order to set everything in motion." She goes over to one of the valves and looks at Logan, who's now holding the other. The two nod and begin turning, putting their full strength on them until they move. As they finish up, they back away slowly as the room begins to vibrate. One of the smooth cement walls starts to crack open, and water surges out.

"All right, Jimena, lead the way!" Logan says. Jimena turns and runs, Logan following right after.

Carter feels the rumbling and breaks away from the fight. Without saying anything to the two, he runs away. However, they both notice and start chasing after him. Carter dashes down the tunnel, looking for an exit. He reaches an end where he hopes for an exit when the wall breaks and sprays water everywhere. Carter slides to a stop, assessing the newfound obstacle. He jumps to the side, avoiding a swing from Titan. He turns his head to the right quickly, ducking soon after, avoiding a chop from Lothar.

Carter launches his fist into Lothar, stunning him for a second. Without hesitating, Carter dashes off, slipping on the water for a moment before taking off. As he runs away, he gets slammed to the ground. He flips over and sees Titan on top of him, right about to plunge their sword into Carter's chest. Carter grabs the blade as Titan lowers it down. The blade cuts Carter's hands as he tries to hold it back. The lights in the tunnel go out, and they're now only illuminated by spinning orange warning lights. Carter wrestles the sword out of Titan's hands, flinging it to the side. Titan unleashes a flurry of punches on Carter's face, hitting his mask every single time.

"Titan-listen-to-me-for-a-moment," Carter says between punches. He catches one of Titan's fists and throws them off him, quickly getting up to his feet. Titan gets up from the water-covered floor and points their sword at Carter. Carter's

mask is cracked, with a chunk of it missing from his right eye. He

holds his hand up in front of him, drawing his weapon as the floor

begins to flood. "Listen to me! If we keep fighting, we both will die

and then your efforts will be wasted!" Carter screams through the

sound of rushing water. The two turn to the end of the tunnel to

see a glowing red blade appear from the darkness. "What a

cliche." Carter turns away from Titan to face Lothar.

"You two pests are going to die here!" Lothar says, his

voice booming down the tunnel.

"Look, you either help me defeat him or we can both run

right now and deal with him later," Carter says.

Titan pauses for a moment, then turns to Lothar. "He's too

dangerous to be kept alive. We have to kill him now so he won't

be a problem later." Lothar clicks his tongue and then rushes

toward the two, pulling out another glowing red sword.

All of their movements are slowed by the water as the two being attacked try to get further down the tunnel, away from the source. Lothar pushes Titan to the side, unleashing a whirlwind of strikes on him. He blocks all the swings, but the sheer force pushes Carter into the water. Titan comes back into the fray with a swing, but Lothar blocks it. As Titan tees up another swing, Lothar switches tactics and does the same to Titan as he did to Carter. Lothar keeps swinging his arms around, bashing into Titan's sword until one swing cuts through the sword, breaking it in two. Lothar slashes Titan with the other sword and they fall to the ground with a cut in their armor.

Lothar laughs for a moment, then raises his swords and swiftly plunges down. A clang rings out as the blades are stopped by one of Carter's. Lothar turns just to see Carter bring his other sword across his face. Lothar screams as he stumbles back, dropping one of his glowing swords into the water. The flooded floor hisses from the blades as its glow dims to nothing. Lothar

looks at Carter, clenching his other sword tight as he holds the

side of his head with his other hand.

"What is your plan, Karma? Why save Titan when they'll

just come after you again?"

"Who said I was saving them? I made a promise to destroy

you and your little cult! I will use whoever to get what I want!"

Carter bellows and leaps toward Lothar. The two fight, with each

passing moment growing tenser as the water level rises. Carter

breaks the chain of deflects and uses one sword to smack Lothar's

sword out of the way, then rams the other one through his

stomach. As Lothar stumbles backward with the sword in him, he

raises his arm and moves as fast as he can toward Carter. Carter

pulls out Kismet and shoots him in the leg. Lothar falls to the

ground, leaking blood into the water. He coughs and blood pours

out from the bottom of his mask. Carter puts Kismet away and grabs Lothar by the neck. "You can thank Aubrey for the information on your little base." Carter smirks as Lothar squirms. Carter rips his sword out of Lothar and kicks him over, away from Titan. Lothar bobs in the water as he tries to get air. Titan lies in the water, barely moving. Carter jerks his head back around to see Lothar stumble onto his feet.

"I won't let you get away!" He clenches his sword in his hand and looks at Carter, opposing him. With a wild scream, he moves as fast as he can and leaps into the air. Before he can get close to Carter, the wall cracks open, launching a burst of water at Lothar, knocking him away. The roof above Carter collapses. He jumps out of the way, dodging the falling debris as it blocks the walkway, sealing Carter off from Lothar. Carter lands in the rising water. He takes a few deep breaths and puts his swords away, then stands back up. He trudges through the water back the way he came.

"Karma!" Titan shouts from the tunnel.

"Crap, I thought I had a little more time," Carter says, then starts to look for another way. He eyes the catwalk he started on and jumps into the water. Titan catches up to Carter and sees him swimming away, so they leap onto a bobbing crate.

"Stop running!" Titan shouts as they leap to another floating crate. Carter reaches the supports of the catwalk and climbs out of the water and onto the metal floor.

"Sorry, Titan. If you want to take me down, you'll need to do better than this!" Carter heads in the direction Jimena and Logan went initially.

"Help me!" Titan shouts. Carter stops in his place, listening. "Karma, help me!" Titan's voice becomes less robotic and closer to a human's voice. Carter stares at Titan, lying on top of the box, completely helpless. He clenches his fist and punches the railing.

266

"Dammit!" Carter looks around at all the current hazards. The ground shakes as more water bursts out from the ceiling. Carter's head jerks to the side and he sees a wave of water wash down to him from the other side of the facility. The wave takes Titan deeper, further away from him. After the wave passes, Carter hops onto a crate and rides the remaining momentum down to catch up with Titan. After a few moments, he finds Titan floating in the water. "I'm gonna regret this so much." Carter reaches down and pulls Titan out of the water, slinging them over his back like a bag. "Titan, you need to eat a sandwich. You're so freaking light." Carter jumps into the water and swims to the edge. Titan starts to move. "Hold on tight! And don't you dare try anything!" Carter says as he holds onto a bar attached to the wall. Titan nods and clings onto Carter tighter.

Carter travels back up, moving from whatever he can get a good grip on. They eventually reach another metal catwalk and climb on top of it. He runs into one of the rooms, still carrying Titan on his back. He reaches a point, but gets turned around by collapsing walls and roofs. The water forces them down one final path. The end of the tunnel is filled halfway with water and rising.

"There! An exit hatch has to be up that ladder!" Titan says, pointing at the corner of the path. Carter nods and pushes forward. He reaches the metal bars that form a ladder and begins to climb. They reach the top, where a hatch is sealed above them. Carter pushes on it, but it doesn't budge. The water rises faster as it converges on their tunnel. Carter punches the hatch, hoping it will open. The water crawls up the two and swallows them whole.

Carter takes a deep breath, quickly realizing his mask allows him to breathe. His eyes widen and he takes a few deep breaths before taking the bottom half of his mask off. He reaches behind and grabs Titan's mask. Carter cracks off the bottom half and shoves his mask piece over Titan's mouth. Carter then takes his swords and slams them into the crack of the hatch and pushes. Eventually, it breaks open.

Carter lets go of his swords and pushes on the hatch as he feels his vision fading. He opens it fully, and the water pushes them out of the hatch hole and outside. He gasps for air as he flops onto the ground with Titan on his back. He coughs for a bit and then attempts to get up. Carter feels Titan raise their arm, and he grabs Titan's wrist from over his shoulder, flinging them off his back and across a grassy field.

As Titan flies through the air, they drop something that rolls toward Carter. Carter stands up fully and swipes his hand across his face. His mask reappears, with the crack over his eye almost fully repaired. He walks over to the object—the spider-like drone the scientists were testing back in the labs. He puts it into his coat and walks away, on the lookout for Logan and Jimena.

"You sure took your sweet time." Logan smirks, punching Carter's shoulder.

"Sorry, there was some flash flooding that blocked my path." Carter chuckles, and the three head on their way.

Titan wakes up to the sound of an incoming car. They get to their knees as the car stops and a door opens. Footsteps sound, and Titan raises their hands, placing them on their helmet. The helmet makes a few clicks and then they take it off, releasing long locks of wet hair.

"I take it the mission was not successful?" Mr. Shardlow asks. Titan lowers their head. "Speak."
"Was the business meeting successful?" comes Titan's feminine voice, exposed without the helmet.

"It was, although I'm pretty sure my daughter would appreciate not being bothered by teenage boys horny for the first girl they see." Mr. Shardlow chuckles.

"I'm sorry for failing you. The Heinous Hearts betrayed us, and the Evil Alliance were there as well."

"Keep your chin up. We still have time. For now, rest is in order." Mr. Shardlow walks back to the car and gets into the passenger seat. Titan punches the ground, covering her hand in dirt. She stands up and puts the helmet back on, then gets into the car.

Chapter Seventeen

A few days have passed since they'd flooded the cultist's meeting spot. Carter works on some homework at his desk after a week at school, when Leonidas appears in front of him. "Carter, I have a lead for you."

"Okay, a lead on what? You also can't just pop up and say you got a lead. Actually, now that I say that out loud, that is basically everything you have done up until this point," Carter says, focusing back on his homework.

"I found you a lead to the last Karma."

"That was fast. Why didn't you just start with that?" Carter stares at him.

"Stop nitpicking everything. Do you want to know where he is or not?" Leonidas stares back.

"Yes, go ahead."

"He lives outside of the city in a small town called Berry Grove. It's a very humble town, so when you go, just be considerate."

"More considerate than I normally am?"

"Yes. This is a small town of less than a hundred people. Everyone knows each other. If you do something wrong, the whole town may turn against you. You need to get to him and ask about the immunity to Rood Staal and get out as soon as you can before you say something you shouldn't."

Carter pulls out his phone and searches for the town. "Wait, how will I know who I'm looking for? I can't very well ask everyone I run into."

"Carter, I don't know his name. I just know it's a man. The 26th generation of the Evil Alliance was very secretive. Trust me, it was hard just to find an accurate location."

"He was the Karma who killed his entire team. I'm curious what the full story is?"

"That right there is what's gonna get you killed! Don't bring that up at all!"

"Okay, but how am I gonna know it's him?" Carter asks. Leonidas gets close to Carter and phases his hand through his body. "You will feel it and you will know."

The next morning arrives quickly, and Carter awakes and gathers his things for the journey ahead. He mounts his motorcycle, heading off out of the city, traveling a few hours on the road, passing stops along the way. He eventually turns down a small two-lane road that leaves civilization and into a cove of mountains.

The rocky walls of the mountains begin to smooth as he gets further along the path until the bland beige rocks turn into luscious plains of grass and trees. The mountains fade away as they become flanked by flora on all sides. His eyes lock on the small town in the distance and decelerates until he arrives at the edge of town.

Carter cruises through the quiet streets, passing by small local shops with no distinct names, only words describing what they sell. The majority of the shops have a second floor for the owners' housing. As he rides throughout the town, the few people give him weird looks and side eyes. There are no stoplights, only intermittent stop signs scattered throughout the town with only a few cars parked in front of businesses. Carter pulls over and checks the map on his phone.

"The map isn't gonna help me. Leonidas said I would be able to feel his presence." He looks up and down the road until his gaze lands on a tree stump in its own small garden. Carter drives over to it and parks in a spot outside its small fence. The top of the stump looks like it was sliced off, but amongst the smooth top, new flowers are blooming, with the roots also sprouting flowers of its own.

Carter kneels down and places his hand on the stump. A vision of the previous Karma dueling someone in a black cloak and a Rood Staal sword appears in his mind. He sees Karma disarm the cloaked figure by making them slam the sword into the trunk of the tree. Karma's next two sword swings break the Rood Staal blade in half, leaving the top half still lodged in the tree and the other swing cutting through the trunk, creating the stump that resides here now. Carter opens his eyes and looks to the left to see a woman looking at him. "Can I help you, ma'am?"

"What are you doing, boy?" the woman asks. Carter looks back at the stump and sees the blade is still lodged in the stump. He stands to his feet and dusts off his pants.

"I was curious about the stump. I've never seen a tree cut so smoothly before," Carter says, slowly walking back to his bike.

The woman eyes Carter up and down. "Why are you here?"

"I'm looking for someone … someone who can help me," Carter says.

"Lots of people here can help. What do you need help with?"

"It's not something I can clearly put into words."

The woman shrugs, then begins to walk away. "Best of luck to you."

"Yeah, you too." Carter watches for a moment as the woman shuffles away. He hops back on his bike and rides further into town. Carter enters the housing community. He reaches the center, then feels a tug in his mind. He slides his bike around, following the direction of the pull, and rolls down a street down to a cul-de-sac where he sees kids playing Tee-ball in the street.

Carter parks his bike far enough away from the game. He takes off his jacket and helmet, strapping the folded helmet to his side while stuffing his jacket into his backpack. Carter walks down the sidewalk, feeling the pull getting stronger and stronger with each step. He stops in front of a house, feeling the strongest pull yet. As he stands there, some of the parents begin to watch him, along with a few of the kids. He walks to the door, but stops when he sees a car pull up in front of the house.

A well-dressed man steps out, a gun strapped to his side, and a metal badge on his belt. "Excuse me son, got a call about a suspicious young man. Can I ask what your business here is?"

"I'm looking for someone. I-I need to speak to them." Carter looks down at his shaking hands.

"Son, why don't you come down to the station with me and I can help you find who you're looking for?"

"He's looking for me." A man's voice interjects, causing Carter to whip his head around. Before him stands a pale man in his late thirties, his hair short and burned black, paired with a neatly trimmed beard strapped to his face. His powerful aura matches his bulky physique. The two look at the man and immediately feel his dominating presence over the area.

"Afternoon, Travis. Do you know this kid?"

"I do. I sent him my address, but you know those map apps. They don't like working in our little town. He's also a bit shy, so he was probably too embarrassed to ask for help, so I apologize for his wandering gaze," Travis says, stepping down to stand next to Carter, grabbing hold of his shoulder. "He's a friend from out of town. He was visiting the local area, and I told him to stop by to hang out for a bit."

"All right. I'm glad things are cleared up. Maybe next time you go pick him up from his hotel."

"Don't worry, I will."

"Good. Take care, Travis. Pardon me, kids." The man gets back into his car and drives away, waving to the kids as he goes.

"Come on, Karma. You must have a good reason for being here," Travis says quietly, walking back to his house. Carter follows him inside and shuts the door behind him. "Honey, we have a guest. Could you prepare some drinks?" Travis shouts up a set of stairs.

"Sure thing. Be right there!" a woman says, followed by footsteps.

Travis takes Carter to a table and has him sit down. "I'm sure you're wondering why you no longer feel that pull anymore, huh?"

"I just noticed it's gone," Carter says, putting his hand on his chest.

"It's a hidden power. It allows us to find people like us, people who were once part of the Evil Alliance, as a way to help each other out. Whoever created these powers was smart, that's for sure. And no, I don't know who made them. My guess is some cruel god." Travis chuckles for a second. A woman of Asian descent with long black hair enters the room, carrying a tray with a pitcher of lemonade and four cups.

The woman stands on the tips of her toes and kisses Travis, then sets the tray on the table in front of Carter. She stands up straight, adjusting her long, flowing sky-blue skirt that connects to her wrists. Carter nods his head as he looks her over fully; she has a hibiscus flower tattoo on her left shoulder and two red curvy stripes that run from under her black tank top down past her stomach and under the skirt that contrasts with her cream-colored skin.

"Thank you for welcoming me into your home," Carter says.

"What's your name?" she asks.

"My name is Carter."

"Nice to meet you, Carter. My name is Saige."

"So Carter, what is it you need from me? Don't worry, she knows about what we are," Travis says.

"Oh, are you the new Karma?" Saige asks. Carter nods and stands, making his armor appear, showing it off before it disappears.

"Not as flashy as my outfit, but still nice." Travis smirks, pouring himself a glass of lemonade and taking a sip.

"If you want to stay here to lie low, we won't mind," Saige says, pouring lemonade in two of the other glasses.

"I appreciate your offer, but not that kind of help."

"You need my help fighting?" Travis asks.

"I would love that, but you have your own life, and I'm not dragging you into my fight. I need to know what your special counter was."

Travis stops mid-sip. "I'm assuming you're asking because those damn cultists don't know when to quit, do they?" He sets his glass down.

"Partially, yes. I've had a run-in with them, and even infiltrated one of their hideouts, but my problem is with their supplier."

"Their supplier?"

"Well, ex-supplier. I kinda helped them sever their partnership. Their supplier is a company called Iron Works, but they go by Iron Organization when it comes to their hijinks."

"I didn't know they had a supplier that wasn't just another branch of their weird dominion." Travis rubs his chin.

"That's why I need your help. I can't keep fighting both of them if they're going to have a constant advantage over me and my teammates. I need to know how you fought back."

"Look, Carter, I understand how you feel. Having to fight an uphill battle is not easy, especially with your own life on the line. My best advice for you is to stay out of most of it."

"You mean give up? Stop fighting? Just let them get away with what they're doing?!"

Saige goes over to him and grabs his shoulders gently. "Carter, you should listen to what Travis is saying. Stop fighting. I can already tell you aren't one to give up, especially if you came all this way just for help. You are young, you have your whole life ahead of you. You shouldn't be wasting your youth fighting a war." Saige gives him a smile and lets go of his shoulders.

"I'm not fighting for the sake of the world or my city. I'm fighting to protect my best friend. She's the daughter of Iron Works's CEO. He is a kind man, but he clearly has ulterior motives. I don't want to see my friend get wrapped up in all of it."

"Oh Carter, that's very noble, but there has to be some other way to deal with this instead of just brute force." Saige locks her green eyes with Carter's blue ones.

"We've tried. Mr. Shardlow is a clever man and is very thorough. He leaves nothing behind that can be used against him." Carter lowers his head in defeat, clenching his fists.

Saige turns and looks at Travis. He sighs and rubs his face, groaning. "All right, listen. What I did was not something smart. It could have killed me if I was reckless with it," Travis says as Carter looks up at him. "I made myself immune to the effects of Rood Staal."

"You did? How?!"

"Relax, okay? My immunity wasn't something that just happened. Also, it only started as a resistance to it. I had to inject myself with Rood Staal slowly until it stopped having an effect on me. Not a fun process. It's very painful, even with our pain resistance. Not to mention, it wasn't permanent. At most, the effects lasted a month."

"That's really it?" Carter tilts his head.

"Is that it?! Yeah, that's it. I just told you it's a very painful process, and you're just fine with that?"

"I mean, yeah. Honestly, I expected worse." Carter shrugs his shoulders, smirking.

Travis rubs the bridge of his nose while looking up, sighing deeply. "Come with me." He leads Carter outside to a large open field behind the house with no fences separating the houses. Travis picks up a few baseball-sized rocks and hands one to Carter.

"What's this for?"

"Throw it as hard as you can at that tree way over there." Travis points to a tree about thirty yards away. Carter preps himself, then takes a few steps forward, throwing the rock. It flies through the air like a bullet. It hits a small branch on the tree and breaks it off. Travis smirks, then throws a rock himself. It too flies

fast and breaks another branch on the tree.

"What? You still have powers?" Carter's eyes widen.

"You aren't aware of that rule?"

"What rule?"

"What is most commonly known about the powers of the

Evil Alliance is that only one person can have the powers at a time

for each designation. While yes, that is primarily true, it's also not

at the same time."

"What do you mean?"

"When you are an active member of the Evil Alliance, your

access to those powers are unlimited, meaning you can use the

abilities and summon the armor and weapons freely. But once you

cut yourself off or retire the powers, you lose that connection and

are left with whatever your body can hold. So while yes, I still have

my powers, I cannot regenerate them. My physical abilities still remain and will forever remain, although they have dulled." Travis puts his finger on Carter's chest. "This won't be leaving you. Your body's DNA has basically become altered or enhanced to be capable of using magic. That is permanent. The Devil from the generation before me was nearly a hundred years old, and he was in great shape. He didn't pass for another decade after I met him." Travis moves his hand to Carter's shoulder.

"This is all news to me. My father's research only said there can be one at a time, nothing about a connection or anything like that. So wait … you can still use your Karma powers?"

"Yes, I can, although my time with it is short. If I use one aspect of it at a time, I have maybe a day's worth of it, two if I'm lucky. But If I were to go all out, it would be gone within three hours."

"I'm assuming you're saving those three hours in case of an emergency? Not to blow it on helping some kid with his personal problem." Carter smirks.

"If I had more time, I would help you, but I don't. Now, as a member of the Evil Alliance, your powers will grow and advance with time, but they cannot be unlocked until you are ready for them. Your body is something you need to strengthen. The stronger you are, the stronger your powers will be. It's also not just physical strength. When I evolved, I had a moment of mental maturity, if you will. At that point, that's when I became stronger."

"So what you're saying is that by getting stronger as a person, I can become more powerful with my abilities?" Carter scratches his head.

"Exactly! Also, as a quick tip for you, try to have an extra weapon on hand. In case your powers are temporarily shut off by Rood Staal."

"So something like this?" Carter says as he reaches to his side and pulls out Kismet, holding it out to Travis.

"Is that my gun?"

"You were the one who requested it be made. I think it's only fair that it belongs to you. I can get a different one." Travis looks at the pistol, then back to Carter. He takes it from his hand and looks at it, admiring the quality of Darius' work.

"How did you get this?"

"I tried to save Darius' friend from the Heinous Hearts. He gave me what I needed to meet with him. I returned his gun to Darius and had a chat with him. He didn't sell you out. I had my own way of finding your general location. But Darius gave Kismet to me, saying it would be more useful in my hands instead of collecting dust." Carter scratches his neck.

Travis runs his fingers across the name branded on the gun. "I had Darius make this for me just before the event. But

290

after everything that happened, I decided to leave it with him, saying if I needed it, I would come back for it. Obviously, that day never came. So you can keep it. Like Darius said, it would be of greater use in your hands." Travis holds it back out to Carter.

"I, um … Thank you, Travis." Carter takes it back and puts it away.

"Don't mention it. Now, if you're serious about gaining immunity against Rood Staal, we'll need to get our hands on some pure material." Travis opens the door to the house, with Carter quickly following.

"I have accumulated some of their weaponry, including a sword made purely of Rood Staal," Carter says.

"That won't be enough."

"Hey, you two. Go wash up and get ready for dinner," Saige says.

"Oh, I can't possibly stay for dinner. I've already stayed long enough."

"Nonsense, please stay. I won't allow you to leave without eating. Now go wash up!" Saige says.

"I would just do as she says." Travis smiles and leaves the room. Carter goes upstairs and washes his hands in the bathroom. When he comes out, he sees a little girl standing in the doorway, bearing an uncanny resemblance to Saige.

"Hello there." Carter smiles at her.

"Hello. What's your name, mister?"

Carter crouches down. "My name's Carter. What about you?"

"Tricia." She smiles back at him.

"Well Tricia, how about I help you wash your hands and then we will go eat dinner? Sound good?"

"Yeah!" Tricia says, bouncing. Carter helps her out, and they go back downstairs to join the other two. They all have dinner and enjoy each other's company.

Afterwards, Carter and Travis go into an office. Travis goes into a cabinet and pulls out a cardboard box. He rummages around in it and then pulls out a small wooden box and opens it, revealing a handful of red dust and pebbles of the same color. "Unfortunately, I don't have enough to make you immune. And the weapons you said you've collected, although they contain the mineral, are not pure. They learned that a blade made out of pure Rood Staal is actually not very strong, so they have to make an alloy that consists of at least equal parts Rood Staal and steel."

"Wait, if Rood Staal is just red steel, why is it so weak compared to normal steel?" Carter asks, swiping his finger through the dust.

"Honestly, I don't know. I didn't name it. Regardless, there's a stump in town that has a chunk of a sword still in it. No one can pull it out, so they left it as a kind of mini tourist attraction. You can take it and break it down into a dust like this, then mix it with blood and inject it back into your system. I found that the batches where the dust was at its finest or in a liquid form worked faster," Travis says, putting the lid back on the box and handing it to Carter. "I've told you what I know. You seem like a smart kid, so I'm sure you shouldn't have any issues with this."

"I don't know what to say, Travis."

"Oh right, I should give you some more advice. You may have noticed that any damage to your armor gets repaired after some time, but you can make it go faster at a cost," Travis says, recalling his past. "You can make your armor disappear, still leaving your weapons and the basics behind. By doing so, the armor you're currently using will repair faster."

"Really?" Carter activates his armor and looks at it while setting the box down. "But how do I take it off?"

"Once you understand the process more, you'll be able to do it with just a thought. For now, act as if you were going to take that coat of yours off." Travis moves his arms, imitating the action he suggested. Carter grabs hold of his coat and begins to pull on it. Upon pulling it far enough, the entire coat disappears, showing off the full silver armor plate on his chest and the brown leather straps it's attached to, slung over a simple gray shirt. Alongside the disappearance of the coat, the belts that run across his chest that hold his swords' sheaths tighten, filling the gap left by the coat.

"Whoa, that's cool." Carter looks at himself with a shimmer of excitement in his eyes.

"Simply act as if you were going to put the coat on and it will reappear." Travis once again imitates the action. Carter follows, and his coat glows back into existence, with the rest of his armor going back to its original state.

"If I remember more things, I'll let you know the next time we meet. Now then, I wish you the best of luck, Carter." Travis holds out his hand. Carter's armor disappears and Carter grabs his hand and shakes it.

"I … I can't thank you enough. This is a lot of helpful information."

Travis smiles. "Don't mention it. Just keep the world safe, is all I ask."

"Can I ask you an awkward question?" Carter says, picking the box up.

"Is it about what happened to my team?"

"Yeah, it is. You see, my father is the reason I was so involved in the Evil Alliance, and it's thanks to his research that I was able to come into possession of these powers. One of the things I was most unfamiliar with is the truth of your team's

death," Carter says, looking down at the box.

"How about I tell you the quick version and you come back

another day and I can give you the full details? Start to finish.

Sound like a deal?" Travis holds out his hand.

Carter shakes it. "Deal."

"All right. Well, to start at the root of the situation, it was

the government that wanted to move in and take the power as

theirs as they believed because the temple is somewhere on

American soil that it's theirs. But after that plan didn't go well,

they tried to make a deal with us to assist them in black ops

missions. After our refusal, they were approached by the Heinous

Hearts, who promised they could aid them in apprehending us

and having us work under the government's rule. What the

government rushed into was actually worse than they could have

imagined. The cultists gave them weapons to stun us, but it was all to capture and mind control us. I knew what was happening because I saw it happen to my team's Curse. She didn't stand a chance. I escaped while I could, and when I received an invitation from her to meet up at our hideout, I knew that if I refused, they were going to harm my friends."

Travis takes a deep breath and clenches his fists. "When I got there, they all raised their arms to take me down and make me subdue. The night I got that message is when I began to undergo the treatment to make myself immune. It wasn't effective enough to prevent damage, but they couldn't control me. So while the other four had lowered their guards because they thought they won, that's when I struck back. I tried to subdue them myself, but it wasn't happening. I realized in that moment that if I even escaped, the amount of damage they could have done with the four other members was too great of a risk. I took that burden into my own hands and decided to end it myself. I killed them all;

298

it was my only option at the time. After that, I destroyed what the government had discovered and crushed them and their associates beneath my feet. I threatened them to never try it again, but they were determined to get me. I wiped their system of any trace of the Evil Alliance and their identities. And while I was on my way to return the powers, I noticed one of my neighbors was following me. I approached them and discovered they were a spy. I ended their life and returned the powers before they could send another spy while I was still near the temple."

Travis looks over to Carter. "You need to be extra careful to not get caught." As Travis finishes, a knock on the door comes. The two turn to see Tricia standing near the door.

"Dad, can I get a—" She stops and stares at Carter, waving at him.

Travis bends down to get to her eye level. "Tricia, go get your mother and get outside." She nods quickly and rushes down the hall.

"You feel that, don't you?" Carter puts the box into his backpack.

"Look outside." Travis walks over to a window and opens the blinds slowly. Carter peeks outside and sees government vehicles outside, from police to an armored vehicle with people carrying large guns in front of an orange-colored sky. "I had a feeling they put another spy in town."

"It doesn't look like they've identified my bike yet, so I can get to it and ride off," Carter says.

"Go out the back door and run across the backyards. You'll be able to get to your bike that way much easier. I can go out and distract them for a moment, but there's no telling how much it will work. They probably guessed you were a new member of the Evil

Alliance. And since a new team can't form until the original team

has disbanded, they probably put two and two together and

assumed I'm no longer a threat. Now go." Travis waves his hand.

"Thank you again, Travis. I won't let you down," Carter

says, heading out to the back door. Travis walks over to the door,

but it bursts open, landing on top of him. Soldiers covered in dark

clothes slither into houses with rifles in hand. Carter stops at the

door and sees Tricia sitting at the kitchen table with Saige. He

turns and sees a can roll into the room. Carter activates his armor

and quickly grabs a pot on top of the stove and slams it on top of

the can, holding it down with his hand. The pot booms, and one of

the soldiers walks into the room, pointing their gun at Carter. He

quickly kicks the pot at them and they tumble.

Carter rushes over and swiftly disarms them, then lands a

punch across their face. He pulls the table and slides it in the

doorway, then grabs Saige and Tricia, hurrying them outside. "You two need to run. Go to the trees. I'll get Travis." Carter rushes back into the house, kicking the door in himself, knocking down one of the soldiers. He summons his pistol and shoots two others. He leaps over the table into the hallway, shooting the soldiers surrounding Travis. Carter sees more coming to the doorway from outside. He kicks the broken door off Travis and throws it outside, knocking the soldiers over. "Travis, come on. I got your family outside." Carter lifts Travis, carries him outside, and sets him down. "I told them to run toward the trees. Get to them as fast as you can."

Carter turns and rushes into the house again, shooting anyone else who comes in. He makes his way through the house, throwing soldiers around and shooting them. Some of the soldiers fire their guns at Carter, but the bullets fly past him or hit his mask, bouncing off. He rushes past anyone else, making his way outside. He stands on the front lawn, looking at the small army in front of him. Scared families in their homes take peeking glances through their windows.

"Is this how the government works nowadays? Busting into towns and destroying the lives of many all because you're greedy!"

"Silence, criminal! Put your hands up and come with us quietly!" someone shouts from the crowd.

"Fine. I'll leave in that cop car right now if you don't hurt anyone else." Carter holds up his hands and walks slowly toward them.

"Stop what you're doing and get down on the ground!"

"You guys take the fun out of everything." Carter smirks and dashes forward. He weaves in between them and jumps through the window of the police car, and quickly drives off with it. As the car moves, it transforms its colors to black and red, with red lights flashing. As Carter reaches the long straightaway leaving the town, he jumps out, letting the car continue to drive. He hides in a tree as the others chase after the empty car. He runs back to town, heading for the stump. He removes the blade fragment and wastes no time getting on his bike and riding off.

After the sounds have vanished, Travis and his family head back to the house. He tells the two to wait outside while he goes in. When Travis enters, he hears a voice. He picks up one of the rifles off the ground and turns down the hall to see a woman standing there.

"So it was you. I should have known," Travis says. The woman drops a phone and holds up her arms.

"Look, Travis, I have nothing against you. It's just my job, okay? I had no intention for this many people to show up, I swear!"

"You people just don't know when to quit! When will you learn from your mistakes?!" Travis shouts. The woman begins to tear up. Travis kneels down and picks up the phone. "I hope you can hear me, you bastard! I told you to leave me alone, and now you're gonna pay!"

"With what powers? You've clearly passed them along. You're no longer a threat to us."

Travis smiles and looks down at the women before resuming the conversation. "The new Karma has the weapon. So I would be on your toes, and if anything happens to me or my family, they are instructed to use it against you."

"How dare you threaten us! You're not serious, are you?!"

"I'm very serious." Travis lifts the gun and shoots the woman. "Try and send another spy. I know everyone here in town. I won't hesitate to tear this place down just to eradicate you." Travis slams the phone on the ground and destroys it. Saige walks into the house. "I'm sorry, Saige, about all of this."

"Is it true? Does Carter have the weapon?" she asks, grabbing hold of him.

"He does, he just doesn't know it. But he'll find out sooner or later."

Darius Behringer

Chapter Eighteen

Carter stands in front of his table, looking over a chemistry equipment. He moves liquids around, turning knobs and combining liquids. He opens the box he was given and pulls out one of the small pebbles of Rood Staal; he places it into a small vial and swishes it around until the liquid turns to a bloody red. Carter grabs tweezers and plucks the shrunken pebble from the vial, then holds the vial up to the light of the early morning sun.

"I have no idea what I'm doing." Carter sets the vial down on a rack.

Leonidas appears and scolds him. "If you don't know what you're doing, why do you have all of this stuff?"

"I don't see you being a man of science, mister ghost! Besides, this stuff isn't mine, it's my brother's. He's a chemist." Carter goes into a closet and pulls out the Rood Staal Katana, then gets the chunk of sword he removed from the trunk of the tree. He summons his sword and places it on the table, holding it steady. He takes the Katana and swings the blade against his sword with full force. The blade bounces off, but a piece of the blade where it made contact is now missing. He sets the sword down. Leonidas watches in confusion. Carter grabs hold of the blade chunk and swings it against his sword. The whole thing breaks in half, and the half Carter was now holding shatters and splits into more pieces. "Travis was right. Pure Rood Staal is much weaker."

"Well then, how about you call your brother up so you can ask him how to do all of this."

"Leonidas, it ain't that easy. I haven't spoken to him in a long time, and now all of a sudden I'm going to call him up and ask him how to turn a rock into a fluid safe enough to inject myself with." Leonidas smiles at Carter, who sighs and looks at his phone sitting on the table. "Fine, I will give him a call. He scrolls through his contacts until he finds him, then the phone begins to ring.

"Hello?"

"H-Hey, bro. It's been a while."

"Carter? Why the sudden call? Are you okay? Do you need me to come get you?!"

"No, no, I'm okay. I just need help with something only you could help me with."

"Okay … What is it?"

"It's a chemistry thing." Carter holds his chin as he formulates his next words.

"Okay, well, what is it you're trying to do?"

"I need to take a solid mineral and turn it into a liquid, but simply letting it dissolve will take too long."

"Okay, okay. I think I know what you're talking about. Let's see here." A rustling noise fills Carter's ear. "I have a piece of paper ready to write things down. Now, let's begin, shall we?" he says, and the two begin to work over the phone. Carter breaks down more of the Rood Staal as best as he can following his brother's instructions. A few hours later, they get a promising result. Carter holds up a single vial of the Rood Staal liquified.

"We did it!" Carter smiles.

"Good! Now, I've been neglecting my own work, but stay out of trouble and I will talk to you again."

"Thanks, bro!"

"No problem. Bye now." The phone goes silent as Carter looks at the vial.

"What's wrong, Carter?" Leonidas asks, looking confused.

Carter looks at his remaining materials. "There's not enough for all three of us." He sets the vial down on the rack, then He pulls out his phone and makes a call. About a half hour later,

Logan and Jimena show up at his house. The three sit at the table, looking at the vial and syringe.

"So you're telling me this liquid can make us primarily immune to the effects of Rood Staal, but only if we get that one dose completely?" Jimena asks, looking at Carter.

"That's correct."

"Why don't we get more Rood Staal from Iron Works? I'm sure they still have some raw material, even after we destroyed their source," Logan asks.

"For one, we need pure Rood Staal, not from weapons, as those are a mixture of metals. I used a lot trying to just get this. And even if I had the equipment, I don't know how to separate the compounds. So the real question is, who's going to take it?" Carter adjusts himself in his seat. The three sit there in silence as they stare at the vial. Leonidas appears and puts his hand on the table.

"As much as I like you guys making group decisions, there's been a disturbance."

"Do you know where?" Logan asks.

"No, 'cause if I did, I would have told you."

"Thanks, Leonidas. I don't know what we would do without you." Carter rolls his eyes as he gets up. The other two get up and make their way outside. Carter takes the vial and puts it in his jacket pocket, then joins the other two. After a few minutes, they reach the park where they first encountered the Iron Organization. The three armor up as they walk through the park. They look around, then Carter stops and turns to his right.

"Do you see something, Carter?" Logan asks.

"No, but I feel something. Let's go." Carter dashes away. The other two follow in a panic. They stop in front of a cafe and notice a commotion inside.

"Carter, that just looks like angry customers fighting. That's none of our concern," Jimena says, walking away with Logan in tow. He turns, then stops abruptly.

"River!" Carter makes haste across the street to the cafe.

Jimena sighs. "Now it's our concern."

Carter doesn't think twice and jumps through the window, kicking it as it shatters, to see River being held by a large man. Two other burly men turn around holding Dawn, kicking and screaming. Carter clenches his fists and makes a move, only to get a smack on the back of the head, stumbling forward.

"Take the girls! I'll handle him!" The man with the bat starts to spin it around in his hand. The three holding the girls run out of the cafe and get into a van. More men dressed in tank tops and baggy pants appear, all holding weapons of the melee variety. Carter gets to his feet, turning to his attacker. The man with the bat laughs and charges toward Carter, but stops at the sound of a loud bang. The man looks down at his stomach, his shirt turning

red as he falls to the ground. Carter looks up and sees Logan

holding his shotgun. He pumps it and turns to the others who

showed up. Jimena appears next to Logan and pulls out her

pitchfork.

"Get the girls, we'll take care of them!" Jimena shouts to

Carter.

Carter nods and pulls out a wad of cash, then slams it on a

counter. "Sorry about the window!" Carter shouts as he dashes

out the door and onto the street, searching for the van.

Logan puts his shotgun away and draws his axe. "Let's

make this fair, shall we?" Logan chuckles as the two rush toward

the group. He and Jimena beat down and subdue all the men with

ease. "Let's go," Logan says, running in the opposite direction than

Carter went.

Carter eventually catches up to the van, stopped at a red light. The driver looks in the mirror and sees Carter making a break for them. They panic and step on it, launching the van into other cars and into the traffic. Carter jumps from the roofs of cars and grabs onto the traffic light bar and vaults himself over the traffic. In the van, the two girls are tied up with tape over their mouths. Two big men look at them with smiles that reek of disgust.

"Hey, we got a few minutes until the checkpoint. We should have some fun with them," one of them says.

"We aren't getting paid to fuck them, only to capture them and bring them in," the other says. The one gets up and grabs River's jaw, eyes drifting over her body. His big fingers rub across her face as she opens her eyes wide with fear, tears forming in the corners. Dawn watches in pain as she squirms in her bonds, her screams muffled.

316

"This one's got nice hips and a fine ass. It would probably feel great bouncing on my—" The man stops as a blade runs across his throat, a sword protruding through the van's wall from the outside. Blood pours out from the man's throat. Carter rips open the van doors. The other man grabs his weapon and swings it toward Carter, who grabs it and pulls the man toward him, launching them out of the van. The man pouring blood turns around, barely conscious. Carter grabs his head and throws them out as well.

The two girls stare at Carter in his armor with hands covered in blood. He vanishes his sword, then turns to the two girls. "Hold still," Carter says in a gruff voice. He grabs their bonds and cuts them off with his other sword. The girls rip the tape off their mouths. He looks up at the window that leads into the driver's seat. "Move out of the way." Carter raises his fist and sends his hand through the window, grabbing hold of the driver's neck. The girls stare in horror as they hear his neck snap. Carter grabs the two and leaps out of the van just as it begins to swerve. Carter runs away with the two as they watch the van wrap itself around a tree, but soon after, another van charges at them. Carter jumps, but still gets hit, launching the three into the air. As they fly through the air, time seems to slow down. Carter looks around as fast as possible for any solution to their predicament. He sees they're about to fall into a water channel and grabs hold of the two, pulling them in as they land in the water.

Carter opens his eyes, but he can't see much. He touches his face and feels the mask. He starts to sit up, but falls down. His eyes adjust to the sudden change of scenery, taking in the new found darkness. He grunts as he sees a light in the distance approach him.

"He's awake now," the voice says. The light gets in Carter's face and he blocks it with his hands. He moves his other hand, feeling something wet and squishy.

"River, get the light out of his eyes!"

"Oh, sorry," River says nervously. Carter's eyes adjust slightly as she moves the light out of his face so he can see them.

"What happened? Where are we?" Carter asks, trying to sit up, only feeling pain and falling back down.

"We're in the sewers. After we got hit by that van, we fell into the channel and flowed down until we ended up in the gross part. You cushioned our fall with your body," Dawn says.

"That's why I'm sore."

"Yes. River, can you go see if it's safe now?" Dawn asks. River nods and walks away. Dawn starts to stand up, but Carter stops her.

"Dawn, wait!" As the words left his mouth, his eyes widen. Dawn jerks her hand away and grabs a large stick, holding it tightly and dropping her light in the process.

"How do you know my name? I never said my name, only River's!"

Carter tries to sit up again and scoots back, leaning against something solid. He raises his hand and manually takes off his mask. "Dawn, it's okay. It's me. It's Carter." He coughs but he can feel his body healing.

Dawn drops the stick and rushes to his side, placing her hands on his cheeks. "Carter? You're Karma?" Dawn asks, tears escaping her eyes.

"Yes, I am. I know you're going to ask why I didn't tell you, but it's because I didn't want you to get hurt. And yes, I know that's a cliche thing to say."

"I don't care! You're my best friend. We're not supposed to hide things from each other! You said you didn't find it! Was that a lie too?" Dawn says, scolding him and clasping his shoulders.

Carter looks away for a moment. "Look I … I found it by accident. The location I thought I found was actually wrong, and I just happened to find it elsewhere. Listen to me. I don't have much time to explain. Dawn, your father is doing terrible things. He's hurting innocent people just to get my powers. Normally, I would just help him, but what he wants them for is something that can never happen, because nothing good will come of it. You have to trust me on this. I know I'm asking a lot of you, but please believe me." Carter grabs Dawn's hands and holds them tight.

She looks into his eyes as a million thoughts run through her mind. She sheds more tears and hugs him. "I'm sorry, Carter. I didn't know my father has been doing all these terrible things. I'm sorry. If I knew, I would have asked him to stop."

"It's not your fault. He probably kept it from you for a reason." Carter holds her for a moment until they hear River's footsteps coming closer; he lets go and puts his mask back on. Dawn helps him to his feet.

River turns the corner and sees the two. "Good, he's on his feet. It's safe. Your father is here, Dawn,"

"He is?" Dawn perks up.

"Yep." River leads them through the sewer until they see the light from outside. The three step into the light of the setting sun, then Dawn rushes to her father and the two embrace.

"Thank you, Karma." River smiles, then retreats over to Dawn while Carter stands at the exit of the channel. Multiple guards stand around them, weapons in hand. Mr. Shardlow walks down to Carter and stops in front of him.

"What do you want?" Carter asks.

"This is the only time I will let you walk out of here safely. And that is only for saving my daughter. But I assure you, next time we meet, you'll be leaving in a body bag. Do you understand, Karma?"

"And what's stopping me from killing you right now?"

"You think you can win in your current situation?" Mr. Shardlow laughs.

"Yes." Carter's voice deepens and sends a shiver down his spine. He then backs away slowly as Dawn comes down to Carter with a STIM pack and injects Carter, restoring his energy. "Thank you."

"You're welcome. Thank you for saving me and my friend." Dawn smiles at him, then rushes back to River. "Come on, River. Let's go back to my place and we can take a bath together."

"Wait *together* together?" River asks, flustered as she's rushed into the car. Mr. Shardlow leaves, and after a few moments, everyone is gone and Carter is alone. He deactivates his armor and reaches into his jacket pocket, pulling out the vial. He meets back up with Logan and Jimena and explains the plan, and they all go their separate ways afterwards.

Carter goes home and showers. Afterwards, he sits at the table and holds out his left arm. He takes a tight rope and ties it around his arm to make a vein more apparent, then wipes it with an antiseptic wipe. He lines up the eye of the syringe with his vein.

Carter slowly pierces his skin with the needle and then injects the Rood Staal, screaming in pain the entire time. Once he's done, he stumbles to his bedroom, where he collapses on his bed and passes out.

Chapter Nineteen

Carter opens his eyes slowly and sits up, stretching as the morning sun creeps through the curtains, illuminating only a sliver of the room. He takes a deep breath, grabs his prepared gear, then ties a jacket around his waist slightly sideways, covering his right side. He texts Logan and Jimena and then makes his way to school like any other day. Upon arriving at school, he doesn't see Dawn at all. Carter goes through the day, constantly monitoring everyone and everything.

"Crap! I'm late for my next class!" Carter shouts, setting off in a run. He reaches a flight of stairs and makes his way up, running into Dawn at the top. "Oh hey, Dawn. How are you feeling? I got worried this morning after not seeing you." Dawn hugs Carter tightly and begins to cry.

"Carter, I'm sorry. I'm sorry. I talked to him and he admitted everything he's done; all the attacks, the true intentions of his plans, everything! He even rambled about some wish you could have granted!" Dawn cries.

"Hey, hey, hey. You're okay. I'll protect you. I'll make sure he doesn't hurt you—Ugh!" Carter grunts and falls down the stairs. When he reaches the bottom, he sits up and notices a fresh gash on his side.

"I'm sorry to do this, Carter. He threatened to kill you if I didn't bring you in myself. Please come with me peacefully and you won't have to die." Dawn's face continues to leak out tears.

Carter grunts, clenching his fists before erupting in laughter. "You can drop the act. I knew you would do that."

"What are you talking about? I have to do this, okay?"

"Yeah, sure. That's what you want me to think. I knew what you were going to do." Carter rubs his side, looking at the wound.

"What? You knew I was going to attack you?" Dawn shouts.

Carter jumps to his feet. "You're a bad liar." He smirks and stretches the side that was stabbed.

Dawn notices it's completely healed. "How did your wound heal so fast?"

"I've been preparing for this fight. It's the same thing you've done to remain off my radar."

"No. No, you don't mean—"

"That's right, Dawn. A Rood Staal blood infusion. When normal people get one, they're merely undetectable by magic, or at least enough to where I cannot sense the karma of you and your father, but when I do it, I become resistant to its effects."

Carter smiles. "You probably know this already, but the effects aren't permanent." Carter looks at Dawn as her face is struck pale.

"You knew I was part of all of this when you revealed yourself to me."

"Yep. I was curious at first about why I couldn't read your karma at all when we were together. I shrugged it off as me simply not being skilled enough or you didn't have any noteworthy karma, but when I noticed a little bit of karma the day before you and your father's monthly 'doctor' visit, things didn't seem right. Then I discovered the transfusion process and it all became clear to me. You're involved in his schemes at a deep level, so all I had to do was reveal myself to you. I knew after that, it was only a matter of time until you made your move, or better yet, when your father wanted you to."

"If you figured out I was going to do this, why didn't you kill me when you had the chance?" Dawn asks.

"Because I hoped there was a part of you that didn't want to be a part of it, and that you would come clean to me, but now I see I was foolish for believing in my best friend." Carter adjusts his stance as he prepares for a fight.

Dawn clenches her fists tightly and rubs the tears from her face. "It's too late now, Carter. We have strengthened our power, so there's nothing you can do to stop us."

"I beg to differ." Carter grabs the jacket on his side, twisting it to the other hip, revealing Kismet resting in its holster. Dawn's eyes widen as Carter draws his gun and shoots her twice. She falls down the rest of the stairs and lands on the ground. Carter activates his armor, concealing his identity as teachers come out of the room to investigate. Once they understand what is going on, they rush back to their classrooms, and moments later, an announcement is made alerting everyone to stay in their rooms.

Dawn struggles to stand up, leaning against the rails. "That's it. I'm not taking you in alive. I'm going to bring your corpse to my father. Come to me, Titan!" Dawn shouts. A metal box flies through the air and hovers next to Dawn. She stands up straight, and the box unfolds and attaches itself to her, transforming her into Titan. As the transformation completes, Carter notices a container of green STIM fluid attached to her left wrist. She stretches her body as her wounds begin to heal from the fluid.

"So I was right; you're Titan," Carter says as Dawn reaches to her back and detaches a sheath, drawing out a Rood Staal Katana. She screams and leaps toward him. "Bring it on, Dawn. I beat you once. I will do it again!" Carter shouts, blocking her opening strike. Dawn attacks with rough, wild swings, but Carter dodges them easily.

"Die, you thief!" Dawn screams. "Why do you have to be the one with these powers? Why does the one I love have to be my enemy?" Dawn cries. Carter holds Kismet tight; it radiates a deep red glow as Karma's Curse takes hold. Dawn swings downward. He flips his gun around and holds it so the barrel is under his arm, pointing backwards. He moves his arm and blocks the blade with the gun.

"Dawn, you can stop right now and help me stop your father. I don't want fighting you to be the only solution!"

"Shut up! This is hard enough for me as is." Dawn shoves Carter back, then holds her right arm up as lasers fire out of a wrist-mounted device. The lasers hit him, and he stumbles back.

"Damn, that's new. I must admit, Dawn, you really upped your fire power. Unfortunately for you ..." Carter pulls out the STIM pack he stole and stabs it into his arm, injecting only a small portion, then putting it back. "I have tricks up my sleeve."

He takes one of his swords out and rushes back to Dawn. The two clash their blades over and over with Carter firing his gun any chance he gets, wounding Dawn. He takes hold of her and throws her to the side, noticing the container of green STIM liquid on Dawn's arm is half empty already. He runs back to her, throwing his sword, but she deflects it. The blade fades away as it reassembles back in Carter's sheath. Dawn turns back to him just as his leg swings toward her, kicking her in the face before she can react, denting her mask a little. He starts to shoot at her again. Dawn deflects some of the bullets and makes her way closer, lashing at him violently. Carter draws his other sword, barely blocking the attacks. He rolls off to the side and swings the blade, smashing the STIM container.

"No!" Dawn shrieks just before Carter kicks her, launching her down the hall. He chases after her until he reaches the school courtyard and Iron Organization soldiers join the action and begin firing their laser guns at him. He hides behind a table and puts the one sword away. He pulls out his gun and stands up, shooting them down. Before long, they litter the ground, lifeless. He turns to find Dawn but doesn't see her. His head jerks as he hears a large electric hum. He sees another metal box fly into the courtyard similar to the one Dawn summoned earlier, except this one is bulkier. Extruding from the back are large red transparent geometric wings that are almost holographic. Two smaller parts stick out and begin shooting lasers at Carter. He's too late to react and takes every single shot, falling to the ground, covered in wounds. Dazed, he pulls out the STIM pack and injects himself again, draining it to almost empty.

Damn, that hurt. That probably would have killed me if it wasn't for that infusion. Carter gets up and sees Dawn climbing onto the box as it too wraps around her, strapping her in. The metal box unfolds all of its weapons while keeping her airborne.

Two large mechanized sheaths rest on her sides, one with a blade and the other empty. She slides her current sword into the empty sheath and pulls it back out, revealing its transformation into a bigger blade, sparking with energy.

"That can't be good." Carter looks at the sword in the other sheath. "That's Vermillion; I thought she would never use it." He stands up and begins shooting at Dawn. She holds the sword in front of her and the bullets vaporize before they even touch the blade. She retaliates by firing lasers back at him. He dodges out of the way and picks up a large rifle dropped by one of the soldiers, firing lasers at her, making contact with the blade and even her armor. He lets go of the trigger and ducks back down.

"Stop hiding!" Dawn swings the sword, and the blade cuts through everything it touches, barely missing Carter. He dashes and grabs another gun off a fallen soldier, holding down the trigger. Once it's out of ammo, he throws it at Dawn and she destroys it with a swing. She lowers the sword and looks around.

"Where did you go?!" Carter jumps from the second story onto

Dawn's back, bashing away at her wings. She spins her body,

flinging Carter off, cutting him with her sword in the process.

"Danggit." Dawn adjusts her body, and the armor begins to float

higher before it shakes and drops in height. She raises her other

arm to inspect a panel. "Dammit, he damaged my flight core.

Where is my backup?!"

"The other members of the Evil Alliance are stalling us! We

can't get to you!" says a voice over a radio.

"Damn. Fine, I'll do it myself." Dawn readies her sword,

waiting for Carter.

Carter coughs as he tries to get up. He pulls out the STIM

pack and injects the rest into him without realizing he used the

last portion. He takes a deep breath, draws both swords, and leaps

off the roof. He then throws both of his swords, missing Dawn intentionally. She gets distracted by the swords and spins around to find Carter holding a shotgun. He fires, launching a flat line of energy out of it. Carter runs around her as she swings, breaking everything in her way. He retrieves his swords while rolling away from a swing, then gets in front of Dawn and plants his feet. Dawn smirks under her mask and swings the sword down fast. Carter crosses his swords, blocking the attack.

"I won't ask again, Dawn! Stop right now and we can put an end to all of this!"

"No! We need the power of the Evil Alliance to bring my mother back! Join me and we can bring your parents back too!" Dawn shouts as her sword radiates more energy. The power pushes Carter to his knees.

"You need to move on, Dawn! Both you and your father!" Carter breaks the stalemate and looks at her. "I understand your pain! You know I do! But bringing her back won't change anything!"

"Don't try to weasel out of this! She was taken from this world unjustly!"

"I know … Believe me, I know. Your mother was an amazing woman. Someone who took care of me when my parents couldn't. She loved you so much. She would hate to see what you two have done. I don't want to see her face when she learns what you did to your best friend. So I will not join you. I will not stand by your side!" Carter clenches his swords tighter as he stands his ground against his dear friend.

"Then you shall die so that my mother can live!" Dawn swings the sword again, nearly crushing Carter.

"Are you sure that's what your mother would want? Wasn't she the one who told you not to take from others just to make her happy? Just like you did with my ice cream years ago?"

Carter asks.

"I— Stop trying to distract me!" Dawn swings violently, and

Carter blocks as best he can until their blades lock once again.

"Please stop making this hard for me!"

"I'm not making it hard for you! I'm telling you the truth!

Nothing good will come of this! You have to listen to me! I don't

want to fight you. This is not how we should solve this! We can

take down what your father has created. There is still time!"

"Just stop, Carter, please!"

"Not unless you join me in stopping your father!"

"I won't! I *can't!*"

"So be it. I wish I didn't have to use this, but you've left me

no choice! I'm sorry, Dawn." Carter takes a deep breath and closes

his eyes, holding the swords in place. He makes his mask

disappear, then bashes the sword away, tossing his own onto the ground. Dawn swings the sword, but it stops in place in Carter's hand. The radiating energy moves down to Carter's hand and he grunts in pain.

"What are you doing?!"

"Using the dark side of my power to show you the horrors that come with this burden!" Carter screams in pain as the energy travels down his entire arm. The sword's energy fades away as it travels down into Carter. Any red in his armor now glows brightly along with having a fiery like aura. Carter stares at Dawn as his brilliant blue eyes begin to glow as well. He shoves the large sword off to the side and moves in a blur. His sword vanishes from the ground and then Vermillion disappears from Dawn's side. He reappears in front of Dawn, holding the mechanical sheath before tossing it to the roof of the school.

Dawn becomes enraged and swings her sword. Carter retaliates, breaking her sword in half. The laser guns reappear in response and begin firing. Carter blocks every shot, the blasts bouncing all over the place with some of them hitting Dawn. Carter vanishes again and reappears in front of her. He rips Dawn out of the armor and begins tearing the suit apart, destroying everything. He breaks open the back and finds a container full of STIM fluid. He smashes it, the green fluid spilling out over the ground.

Dawn crawls away in fear. Carter stops his rampage of destruction, turns, and sees her running. Without thinking, he throws his sword at her. It glides through the air and hits its mark. The blade pierces Dawn's chest, impaling her. She looks down at the blade, her face growing pale as she tries to lift her hands. Carter stands there, breathing heavily as his lust for destruction fades. He turns his head toward her as panic takes over. He dashes over to Dawn as she falls to the ground. Carter slides and catches her in his arms before she hits the ground.

"I-I'm …" Dawn's voice cracks as she clings to each breath.

"No, no, no. Dawn, don't talk. Stay with me, okay? Just keep your eyes on me!" Carter takes off Dawn's helmet and looks into her weary eyes. He sets her down and pulls out the STIM pack, but sees it's empty, and only a few salvageable drops remain of hers. He collects them in the empty pack and rushes back over to her. He grabs the sword, and it vanishes. Carter then shoves the needle into her body near the wound and injects the few drops of STIM. Her body begins to heal, but only a small portion of the wound. Blood continues to pour onto Carter's pants, contrasting with the black material. "Please, Dawn, please!"

"Carter, I'm sorry. I … I should have just listened to you from the start. I was just so … I just wanted to make everyone happy. I just wanted to see my mother again, but it looks like I can't." Dawn forces a smile. Carter's head darts around, looking at the dead soldiers scattered about. He rushes over to each one, checking for STIM packs. Every one he checks is either broken open or used up.

"Dawn, hold on. I'll get you to your father and get you more STIM. You can make it! You have to! You can't leave me yet! Not now, not here!"

"Carter, it's okay. I know you'll find someone to take my place. You're more than just my friend. You were always at my side, always making sure I was all right. It's my fault things ended this way. You … are a … lodestar. My hero …" Dawn raises her hand and touches Carter's face. He holds her hand, tears flooding his eyes. She smiles as her eyes fade and lose focus. He shakes her and tries to get her snap back, but nothing is working. His face goes pale, and he screams in pain, tears coming fast and hard.

"No, no, *no!*" Carter cries out. "Wait, my DNA Is programmed to heal! So I can just—" He rolls up one of his sleeves and angles his sword against it. He slices his arm and a few drops of blood drip out onto Dawn's body. "I need more!" He presses his sword deeper into his arm until the blade trails blood down to Dawn's wound. "Come on, Dawn. Wake up, please!" He shakes her, fists clenched and face wet. He cries for his friend as he begs for her to come back to him. Doors open as the sounds of war disappear and give way to Carter's screams. His mask reappears on his face as teachers and students leak into the halls, school police stepping in and moving toward Carter.

They surround him, guns in their hands. "Karma, don't move!"

River breaks through the crowd. She covers her mouth and tears run down her face at the sight of Dawn's body.

"Oh god! I need to find Carter." River looks through the crowd, trying to find him. One of the officers bend down to grab Dawn.

"Don't touch her!" Carter's voice shakes the air, making the atmosphere tense. He picks up the blood-covered sword and points it at the one police officer like a cornered beast. "Stay the fuck away or I'll kill you all!" Carter's voice attacks the air, striking fear in all who hear it.

One officer steps forward. "Drop your weapon!"

"You think I'm scared of you?! I'll cut you down like a damn fish!"

"Drop your weapon or we'll open fire!"

The crowd backs away into the classrooms again. River lingers until a teacher pulls her into a classroom. Carter sighs and drops his sword. As it lands on the ground, Dawn's blood splatters on the floor. The police move closer, lowering their weapons. They pull out handcuffs and attach them to his wrists. All but one turn away from Carter. He stares at them and breaks the handcuffs. They raise their gun to shoot Carter, but he's already out of the way and knocks the gun out of their hand. He picks Dawn up and

dashes out of the school. The police chase after him, but he pulls

out his gun and shoots every single one of them in the leg, causing

them all to fall to the ground. Carter keeps running, leaving

everyone behind, before his phone rings.

"Logan, you and Jimena meet me at Iron Works

headquarters. We're going to finish this!"

Travis Abney

Chapter Twenty

Carter reaches Iron Works Headquarters in just a few minutes. He bursts through the front door and starts blasting guards before they have a chance to draw their weapons. Logan appears on Carter's left, holding his shotgun. Jimena joins on the right with her rifle.

Logan looks at Dawn, then to him. "I'm sorry it had to come to this, Carter."

"It's fine. I just have some business to take care of. You two know what to do." Carter walks deeper into the building while Logan and Jimena split up. As they travel through the lobby, guards appear and ready their weapons, but are all stopped by Logan and Jimena. Carter reaches the elevator at the back of the lobby and ascends to the top floor. He steps out into a small room with a few chairs and an empty receptionist's desk. He kicks open a set of double doors blocking his way.

"I said not to disturb me. I have no meetings today, and I'm very busy, so what do you want?!" Mr. Shardlow shouts, looking out the window. He turns around and sees the horror in front of him. "Dawn! Put her down!" Carter walks over to his desk and lays her down on top of it. Mr. Shardlow stumbles over as his knees shake. "How could you do this to her? She's just a kid!" He sobs, holding Dawn's hand tightly.

"Don't look at me like I'm the bad guy here. You dragged your daughter into this and now she's gone. This is a result of your actions. Wouldn't you call that karma?"

"Don't spout your lies and propaganda!" Mr. Shardlow stands up tall and clenches his fists while tears trail down his cheeks. "You are nothing but a coward hiding behind a mask trying to act like a hero when you're nothing but a killer trying to claim what he does is in the name of justice!"

"I never said I was a hero, nor am I doing this for justice." Carter sighs, then turns to the door before stopping and facing the two again. "There will be certain individuals you meet in your life that just stick out more than others, and those are the people you want by your side regardless of the reason, because making them your enemy would be one of your biggest regrets." Mr Shardlow's eyes widen and his legs begin to wobble. He falls to the floor, his heartbeat accelerated. Carter removes his mask, and Mr. Shardlow becomes horror-stricken at the sight. He shakes his head, trying to imagine it was someone else.

"Carter … It was you. You killed her. She cared about you so much. She would even—"

"Die for me. Look where that got her," Carter says, grabbing his pistol. Mr. Shardlow climbs into his chair, holding his head in his hands.

"What do you think killing me will solve? Will it bring your parents back? Get justice for Dawn? Tell me, Carter. Tell me!" Mr. Shardlow slams his hand on the desk.

"I have nothing to gain. Right now, my companions are exposing all the deals and operations you swept under the rug. And once that goes public, your company and any others with significant tie-ins with your world-ending endeavors will be arrested and their businesses terminated along with it." Carter steps closer to the desk. "As for you, your death is only a release. You will then be able to see your wife and daughter. If you don't end up in hell." Carter gets his pistol ready. Mr. Shardlow stares at his desk for a moment, lost in thought, only to look up at Carter with a blank stare.

"I must say, you have a point." Mr. Shardlow sighs and kisses his daughter's head. "Okay, I'm ready. Finish this." Mr. Shardlow closes his eyes and takes one last deep breath as Carter puts the gun to his head. He pulls the trigger. Mr. Shardlow opens his eyes and Carter raises his other hand, showing the gun's magazine.

"I may not be a hero, but I will try my best to be one for those who believe I am." Carter starts to walk away, pulling out the spider-like device he got from Titan and throwing it over to Mr. Shardlow. "Good luck." Carter puts his mask back on and leaves. Bodies litter the lobby. He stops at a server room to see Logan standing guard with Jimena typing on a computer. "How's it going?"

"It's almost done, but there are some things we may not want to release." Jimena turns in the chair and shows Carter. "That's that Travis guy, right?"

"They have the old files the government once had. Let me go through everything real quick." The two trade places and Carter transfers the files over to a separate flash drive. "All right, everything else can go public. Logan, let's go and set the charges." The two quickly make their way through the labs below the building and set up the explosives Darius gave them. They regroup with Jimena and exit the building. Moments later, police arrive and prepare to breach the building. As the three stand atop a rooftop overlooking the scene, Carter pulls out the remote and detonates the explosives. The ground shakes, but the building shows no signs of distress. They turn away and leave as the police make their way in.

Chapter Twenty One

"Today, the police finished rounding up all who were associated with Iron Works and their plans to tear down and control the entire United States. There were a total of one hundred forty nine members signed on the project. Leader and CEO, Darson Shardlow, is still missing but deemed to be of no threat for now. His daughter, Dawn Shardlow, was killed the same day of the release of information, at Castle High School in Parabi by the leader of the Evil Alliance, Karma. Thanks to the information release, we learned their plans of hunting down the members of the Evil Alliance and using their abilities as the base of their plan. The remains at Castle High School were a testament to what they could do, with weapons capable of mass destruction. All weapons located on the school's premises were taken by the authorities. The lab these weapons were created in was destroyed by the Evil

Alliance by way of explosive detonation, ensuring nothing would be operational. We are joined by the sheriff of Parabi to get a scoop on the situation."

"Thank you. Right now, all Parabi schools have been shut down until further notice. The events of two days ago were truly alarming, and as police all across the country finish wrapping this up, we are realizing that although we know so much, we now know even less now. Primarily, what was the Evil Alliance's intention in the first place and why would they destroy weapons that could have benefitted us all. Wherever they are, they are welcome to aid us if they follow the rules, but with vigilantes, they'll only help when it benefits them. Some of us down here believe they're hiding something from us, and the only reason they decided to take these matters into their own hands instead of just informing us of the situation is because Iron Works had some dirt on them they don't want us finding out about."

"Thank you, Sheriff. Are there any closing statements you'd like to give us?"

"If you know anything about the Evil Alliance that isn't common knowledge, please let any authorities know."

The TV flicks off and Carter walks out into the garage, turning on the lights. He stares at the car covered by the tarp and then looks to the right at a workbench where Vermillion sits, still encased in the bulky metal sheath. He approaches the bench and pulls out tools to remove the bulky metal. He chisels away at it until the original sheathe is shown, then he undoes the remaining parts that were locking it in place. He takes both the sheathe and blade out of the metal shell and holds it in his hands.

Carter looks above the workbench and sees the spider-like device he gave to Mr. Shardlow encased in foam, plastic, and plexiglass. He takes the sword inside and sets it on the table, his eyes fixing on a blank spot on the wall. He tilts his head, rubbing his chin.

Carter dashes back into the garage and looks around at some bins along the walls until he sees the one he wants, but it's stuck behind the car and he can't get into it unless he moves it. He grabs the tarp, ripping it off and revealing a shiny yet dusty crimson two-door car. He opens the garage, then climbs in the car. He puts in the keys and tries to turn it on but the car just wheezes at him. He does what he can and puts it in neutral and moves the car out the way, grabbing the bin he needs then moves the car back.

"These should do." Carter reaches in and pulls out parts of a wooden sword rack. He takes them inside along with some of his tools, closing the garage in the process. He assembles and puts up the rack. He places both the original Rood Staal Katana he took from Dawn and then Vermillion on the rack, with the handle facing the left and the blades pointing up. He smiles and admires

his work. The front door thumps along with a ring of the doorbell.

Carter raises an eyebrow and opens the door to see a mailman

standing there with a letter in hand.

"I have an urgent letter for Carter Shadson," the mailman

says.

"That's me."

"Here you go, sir. Have a great day." The mailman gives him

a large packed envelope and walks away. Carter shuts the door,

sits down at his table, and looks over the shipping details.

Leonidas appears in front of Carter, taking a seat at the table with

him.

"What's that?" Leonidas asks as Carter's eyes widen.

"It's a letter from Dawn. Did she send this before her

death?" Carter opens it and pulls out the contents. He slides out a

folded piece of paper with writing on it, another paper with less writing, and a key attached to a metal cut out of the Iron Works logo. He grabs the paper with the most writing and starts to read it.

Dear Carter. First, I would like to apologize for not joining you and deciding to go back to my father. I realize that I should have just come to you and then maybe things would be different. Yes, I know I'm going to die. No matter how I look at this, I'll die by either your hands or my own. I'm also sorry I decided to go through with my father's plan to kill you. I was blinded by the loss of my mother and never realized that I just wanted to be cared for. I guess I saw that comfort in you. I'm writing this before our fight, but I know at that moment, I won't change my mind, and that if I go back on the plan, my father won't be happy. Again, I'm sorry for my deeds. I wish I could have spent more time with you. Love, Dawn.

Carter clenches the paper tightly and sets it back on the table.

"She knew I could help. She knew that I could stop him. She knew I would kill her!" Carter stands up and kicks the chair he was sitting in and grabs another one, smashing it on the floor.

"Carter, calm down."

"So why? *Why?!*" Carter falls to his knees. "Why wouldn't she just come to me and tell me everything?"

"There was probably a good reason why, Carter."

"Like what? I'll never know why. I can't ask her." He stands up, clenching his fists tightly. "These powers are not meant for people my age, are they, Leonidas?"

"I, um … They are not." Leonidas turns away.

"Do you know what you have caused, Leonidas? Why did you have to be so cryptic about everything? Why can't you just tell us the truth and fully explain our powers, why did you have to hide everything behind cryptic messages? Was it for your amusement so you can see some kids get themselves killed so responsible people can have the powers again. Is that why you never showed yourself to Travis? Because you knew you didn't have to worry about them?"

"Carter, it's not like that, I swear."

"Are you sure about that? What else are you planning?" Carter shouts, slamming his fist on the table. Just as he does so, the ground shakes and a loud crash is heard outside. Carter activates his armor in response. "What the hell was that?" He dashes to his backyard and spins around, looking for any signs of trouble until his eyes lock on a small crater in the ground. He slowly approaches it and looks inside to find a metallic cylinder container with a deep cyan tint to it. He bends down, and as he picks it up, the container opens up to reveal a necklace resting on a plush red cushion. He takes out the necklace, the chain dropping over his hand. It looks like a silver ornamental coin with a green

gemstone in the center. Carter runs his thumb along the coin and

the gemstone begins to glow a matching green. The necklace flies

to Carter and attaches around his neck. "The hell is this thing?!"

Carter shouts as a glowing green ring appears surrounding him.

The ring rushes up through the air and Carter vanishes from sight.

To Be Continued

EPILOGUE

Boots step across a stone floor, passing blank concrete walls. They turn down another hall and stop in front of metal bars. On the other side of the bars is Aubrey, reading a letter.

"Aubrey Davids," the person says, smacking the bars with a baton. Aubrey looks up to see the guard standing on the other side. He pulls out a key and unlocks the cell door, holding it open. Two other guards appear around the corner. Aubrey folds the letter in her hand and puts it in her shirt pocket. "Come with us." Aubrey moves out of the cell slowly. They shut the door behind them and then begin escorting her. She walks through the halls, watching as others gaze upon her. They take her into a small room with no windows and a table in the middle. The guards leave. Another door opens, and a guard comes in with a box of clothes, setting it on the table.

"Change. When you're done, knock on this door." The guard leaves. Aubrey looks at the clothes, seeing a clean shirt, pair of pants, underwear, and a baggy jacket. She changes out of her prison jumper into the new clothes. She knocks on the door and the guard comes back in with another box. "These are your possessions." He pulls out a few items of value and sets them on the table in front of her. "Oh, and this letter came with your release." Her eyes widen as she takes it. She opens it up and pulls out a slip of paper, reading: *I would go here if I were you*. She pulls out a small key ring and a plastic case with an address in it. After Aubrey gathers her things, she follows the guard into another room, then stops in front of a warden.

"Aubrey Davids, as of today, you are hereby released from Ferrick's Women's Prison and have been pardoned of your crimes. They will see you out." The warden hands over the paper and walks away. Aubrey looks at the paper in awe as she's then escorted to the front gate. She stares at the open road and questions what to do. Just then, a car comes around the corner and pulls up to her. The door on the driver's side opens, and a well-dressed man in a hat steps out of the car.

"Ms. Aubrey Davids, I have been requested to pick you up," he says, opening the back door for her.

"I, um … Who sent you?" Aubrey looks at the man.

"I have been sent by a Mr. Shadson." Aubrey's eyes widen. She nods, then climbs into the car. The man shuts the door quickly, rushing around to get back into the driver's side. "I have been instructed to take you wherever you please."

"Take me here, please." Aubrey shows him the address on the keys. He nods, then begins to drive. Half an hour later, they pull up to an apartment complex. She gets out of the car and looks at the back of the case to see a combination of numbers. She thanks the driver, who leaves soon after. Aubrey walks up to a small gate door with a keypad and punches the numbers in. The door opens, and she goes through. She walks around for a bit until she stumbles upon a door with the matching numbers on the address. She puts the key in and unlocks it, revealing a quaint, semi-furnished apartment.

"Hello, is there anyone here?" She explores the empty home for a moment until she wanders to the kitchen and sees a decorative box on the table with another letter propped up on top of it:

Hello, Aubrey. I know your release was rather sudden and I'm sure unexpected. I'm not going to say that the reason I released you is because I believe you're a good person, but that you can change. You told me you had no intentions of hurting people, and I believe you because I know it's true. Thank you for showing me the way to the Heinous Hearts, by the way. You shouldn't have to worry about them for quite some time.

Hopefully, I can come back to rely on you once again. Good luck, and don't make me regret this or I will personally hunt you down.

Sincerely, Carter.

Aubrey's face grows red as tears run down her face. She sets the letter down and opens the box. Inside the box are bundles of cash and a receipt of rent paid for the next six months. Aubrey's tears flow faster as she falls to the ground, laughing with joy.

www.ingramcontent.com/pod-product-compliance
Lightning Source LLC
Chambersburg PA
CBHW020230010826
48973CB00006B/1446